BARBARIAN'S RESCUE

RUBY DIXON

RUBY DIXON

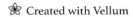 Created with Vellum

BARBARIAN'S RESCUE

BAD DAY? TRY MINE ON FOR SIZE.

ROGUE SLAVERS HAVE LANDED ON THE ICE PLANET AND CAPTURED THE TRIBE. THE ONLY ONES NOT SNATCHED? ME, A WALKING HUMAN MOTORMOUTH WITH NO SKILL EXCEPT THAT OF INCOHERENT BABBLING, AND WARREK, WHO IS AS SILENT AS HE IS ATTRACTIVE. TWO MORE UNLIKELY PEOPLE HAVE NEVER BEEN PAIRED TOGETHER.

AND NOW WE'RE SUPPOSED TO FORM A RESCUE TEAM.

SAVING THE OTHERS IS EITHER GOING TO BRING US CLOSER TOGETHER — OR DRIVE US COMPLETELY APART. I'M PRETTY SURE THE FEELINGS I'M HAVING FOR MY ALIEN COMPANION ARE AS UNREQUITED AS THEY ARE INAPPROPRIATE, BUT SINCE WE AREN'T GOING TO MAKE IT OUT ALIVE, WHAT HARM IS ONE TEENY, TINY KISS?

WHO KNEW THAT ONE KISS COULD CHANGE EVERYTHING?

1

SUMMER

*T*he fruit cave is quiet as heck. I study one of the vines crawling up the high walls of the cave and examine one of the large, juicy pieces of fruit hanging ripe.

It's so quiet I swear I can hear myself thinking. I can hear the water dripping from the leaves. This place is like a hothouse, with the artificial light so far up in the ceiling and a thermal vent somewhere far below. When the others in the tribe first told us that there was a warm cave near the Elders' Ship that was full of lush greenery, I thought it sounded like a fantastic spot to visit. That's why I was quick to volunteer to go fruit picking. Fruit plus warm? Right up this girl's alley.

But I guess I expected birds chirping or jungle noises or something. Anything. Instead, it's so quiet I can hear my own pulse as it beats in my ears.

Not that that's a good thing. I like noise. I like conversation.

And with Warrek? My only company here in the fruit cave? There's neither noise nor conversation.

Part of it is the fact that it's supposed to be several of us heading to this cave to harvest fruit for the entire tribe. Originally, it was going to be Harlow, Rukh, and their son Rukhar leading the way, along with Farli and Mardok, her husband. Mate. Whatever. They were supposed to bring the hunters—Taushen and Warrek —with me and Brooke. Plenty of people around. But then Harlow decided she was too tired and too pregnant to go on the walk and would rather work on the ancient ship. Can't blame her for not wanting to hike while a million months pregnant. And because she bailed, Rukh and Rukhar stayed home, too. I'm fine with that, too, because Rukh's not very chatty or friendly, and his kid is just like him. Then, because Harlow was staying, Mardok wanted to stay behind and work, too. They're busy fussing with something in the old, decrepit ship's controls and seem to be the only two that understand things. I offered to help, but after a few hours of cleaning grease off of parts for Harlow, I've made myself a bit more scarce.

So then Farli decided to stay with Mardok, and it was down to me and Brooke and Taushen and Warrek. Not my favorite, but fruit and a warm cave were still calling to me.

But then Brooke bailed. Said she had a headache. Then said it was cramps. Me, I think she's down with a case of Bullshit-itis and just didn't want to go. Of course, she bailed at the very last minute...which left me with two big strong guys and no buffer.

Some girls would love to be alone with two big hunky dudes all to themselves.

Me? It just makes me nervous, and when I get nervous, I ramble. And, boy, did I ramble on the way here. I have this horrible habit of filling dead air with random conversation. Is it too quiet? Allow me to tell you all about the time I shoved a marble up my nose when I was five. Or how when I first started college, my roommate had lice and I had to burn all of my bedclothes and most of my wardrobe after I found she was borrowing them. Got a spare moment? Allow me to fill your ears with the exciting stories of the last chess tournament I played in.

To say that I fail at small talk is like saying Superman dislikes kryptonite.

At any rate, after about a half-hour of me nattering on in the uncomfortable silence and discussing the optimal non-leather ponytail holders for us on the ice planet when we don't have rubber bands, Taushen decided that he needed to go "scouting" and left.

That meant this trip was basically myself and Warrek.

Ah, Warrek. The person I am least like in the entire tribe. I've never met anyone so quiet. It's like he's got something against noise of any kind. He doesn't make a sound when he walks, always choosing his steps carefully. He doesn't bang baskets around or scrape at his weapons all day long like some of the other hunters. He's always so darn silent.

And talking? Out of the question. I think since we left on this stupid little trip, Warrek's said three words to me. He pointed at the cave and said, "There it is."

That's the extent of conversation I've had in the last day.

I frown at the fruit nearest to my hand and decide to move on, heading for a larger one farther along on the ledge. It's not that there's anything wrong with that fruit, I guess. I'm just distracted by all this peace and quiet.

It sucks.

Warrek's no help. I tried talking to him yesterday when we got here, but he just stares at me with those intense glowing eyes. Worse yet, sometimes he doesn't even look at me. It's like I'm not here, and it makes having a conversation pointless. I never thought I was much of a people person...but I'm definitely not a silence person.

Right now, I'm not even much of a fruit-picking person. I'm very much a let's-just-get-this-over-with-and-go-home sort of person.

I sigh and pick the mango-like pink thing off of a vine and stick it into my woven basket. I don't know how much fruit we're supposed to be picking, so I just keep filling baskets of stuff that looks ripe. Warrek hasn't corrected me on what I'm doing. Heaven forbid he say a word or two. Nope. He just hands me another basket and sends me on my way when I fill one. It makes me grumpy.

Words cost nothing. Why be so stingy with them?

It also makes me grumpy that Taushen abandoned us the moment we set off. As soon as he heard Brooke bailed out, he shut down and took off on his own. I realize Brooke is prettier and has bigger boobs than me, but damn. I like to think that I'm friendly enough that I'm not going to make hanging out with me *that* miserable.

Now I'm stuck with Tall, Blue and Silent in a cave that feels like a sauna, full of fruit that I'm picking instead of eating. On an ice planet in the middle of nowhere.

With zero conversation.

This must be what hell is like.

The sound of my own breathing—and the endless drip drip drip of condensation—gets to be too much. I grab the nearest fruit and look over at my only company.

"What do you suppose this tastes like?" I blurt out as I pull another one of the mango things off the vine. "Tomato? Apple? Pear? I guess you won't know those because those are Earth fruits, but they're kind of sweet and tasty. Well, not the tomato. I guess tomatoes are technically fruit, but they're more acidic and tart and not eaten like fruit. We tend to slice them up and put them in sandwiches and make sauces out of them, which I suppose is kind of like fruit, too. If you think about it, tomato sauce is just like fruit jelly, but on pasta."

Oh god, what the fuck am I even saying?

Shut up, shut up, shut up, Summer!

Warrek just makes a grunt to indicate he's heard me, but doesn't contribute to my inane conversation. Why would he? I sound like an idiot to my own ears. I'm just so tired of the silence, though. There's nothing but the plop of dew falling from the leaves in here and the artificial lights flickering overhead. It's pretty and covered in vines and reminds me of a bird sanctuary from a zoo back at home...minus the birds. I'd welcome birds, because then at least there'd be noise.

A breeze wouldn't be out of place, either. Right now my skin feels hot and slick all over, like I'm taking a really long turn in a wet sauna after a workout. I thought it'd be nice after weeks on end of ice, ice, and more ice, but I forgot that I'd be wearing leather clothing...and that I'd be accompanied by male strangers.

Or, as it turns out, just one male stranger.

Oh god, I hope this isn't some weird way to try and matchmake me and Warrek. Surely there can't be two people less suited to being together than the two of us.

But I can't ignore the idea once it pops in my head.

It's no secret that the reason we were brought here to the ice planet—or as I like to call it, Human Popsicle Planet—because the single hunters of the tiny tribe were in need of girlfriends. Mates, they say, like that makes it sound better.

Thing is, they got the short end of the stick when it comes to me. I'm smart—book smart. I'm also a huge wimp, a worrywart, clumsy, unathletic, and I don't know how to shut up. Which, I suppose, would be fantastic if one of the guys here was looking for a woman who's completely useless and doesn't know when to shut up. But they're not. The few guys that are single are also rather un-chatty, and so I'm probably like nails on a chalkboard to them...not that they know what a chalkboard is.

And really, it's not like I'm begging to be someone's little wifey. The thought's a little insulting.

Okay, it's also a little flattering, too. The awkward chess-loving geek inside me is kind of secretly thrilled at the thought of being someone's sexy, coveted mate. The women here are treated incredibly well by their mates. And they're all ridiculously happy. It's hard not to want that. And the guys are hot. Like seven-foot tall, muscular as all get out, flowing dark hair, every female's fantasy kind of hot. However unpolitically correct it is, it's flattering to think that someone might want me—geeky, verbal-vomit Summer Huang—as their one and only.

Of course, that's not how it works, not really. Even if I found the guy of my dreams, he doesn't get to pick me. The cootie—the symbiont implanted inside us—picks our mates out. Only Gail, who's too old to have more children, seems to be able to pick the guy she wants.

Elly's cootie found her a man right away. That leaves me and Brooke and Kate, and out of the single men? That leaves Warrek, Harrec, and Taushen.

Harrec's obviously got a thing for Kate, so he's out.

Taushen's surly and unpleasant and is clearly not interested.

Warrek? He's silent. Since I'm a yapper, also clearly not interested.

Whatever grand social experiment we're supposed to be contributing to is a big ol' failure on my end. I should have known that even on a planet starving for women, I'd be passed over. Story of my life. No one wants an Asian chick with "personality."

But Warrek still hasn't answered me about how much fruit we need, and I feel frustration start to grow. We don't want to pick too much...or too little. "How many more baskets do we need?" I pause in my plucking and turn around to face my silent companion. "Are we bringing less in since Taushen left? Or do we need to make up his slack and pick some extra? If we do, how are we going to carry it back? I mean, we could always jig a sled of some kind, but I thought this was going to be a quick excursion. I mean, not that quick since we stayed overnight and all, but you get the drift."

Warrek looks up from his careful packing of the fruit and blinks at me with those bright blue glowing eyes. He's unfathomable.

Annnnd he's still silent. God.

"You know what? I'll just go back to picking," I tell him, mentally shooting darts at both his head and mine. Him for being mute, and me for babbling to fill the silence. I'll learn to shut up, someday.

Actually, no, I probably won't. I tend to speak before I think, and that hasn't changed at all in my twenty-two years of life. I don't imagine it'll change anytime soon, either.

Part of me expects Warrek to smile like, "Oh, thank god, she's finally shutting up." Or to just remain completely blank, like a statue. Instead, he cocks his head, animal-like, and gets to his feet, a frown of concern on his face.

"Uh oh, what's going on?" I ask, moving to his side. That's not a good response. I hurry forward as much as I can on the slick stone. The fruit cave has a lot of narrow ledges that mean walking close together or worse, rubbing up against another person. I'm a small woman, but Warrek's definitely not on the petite side. He's all muscle, like all of these hulking aliens, and he's taking up a lot of room on the ledge. I resist the urge to grab at his belt to steady myself when it narrows, and instead hug the vines hanging nearby. "Is it Taushen? What do you hear?"

He puts a finger to his lips, indicating silence, and then heads out to the entrance.

Some answer. Telling me to be quiet? Gee, thanks. Frustrated at that response, I set down my basket and follow behind him. Maybe someone else is showing up soon and I'll have someone else to talk to. I wouldn't even mind Gail and Vaza, though I'm not a big fan of Vaza. He's kind of overbearing, but at least he's sweet to Gail.

I follow a few steps behind Warrek, where he's headed out into the open air, his dark hair fluttering behind him. As I step out onto the hidden ledge, tucked into the side of the cliff, arctic air immediately blasts my flushed face, making my damp hair ice up and my body shiver. I go from sweaty to freezing in a matter of seconds, and not even the thermoregulating cootie can keep up with that. I hug my arms to my chest and peer around Warrek's broad back, trying to see what he's looking at.

A moment later, it becomes obvious. A massive shadow moves slowly through the air, and as I gawk, I realize what it is. I can't believe it.

It's a spaceship.

Not just any spaceship—I'm pretty sure it's the one that bought our group of human slaves and dropped us here to live forever. I'm not an expert on spaceships, but I recognize the sleek length of it, as well as the black metal and the elegant wings that have an almost iridescent shimmer to them. I remember wondering how something so pretty and delicate could travel so far in space.

The ship glides down through the wintry valley and then settles down with a little wobble on the powdery snow. It's landed off into the distance, near where the Elders' Ship is parked, if I don't miss my guess. From our high vantage point in the cliffs, we can see a long way off. While a lot of ice and mountains look the same, I suspect that's the ship's destination. Of course they're going to land by the other ship again. I imagine that they think we'll all be hanging out there.

They're only half-wrong, of course. Our small group went to visit the Elders' Ship, but the rest of the tribe is back in the village down in the canyon. It's several days' hike from here.

"It's the *Tranquil Lady*," I breathe, remembering the name of the spaceship. Holy cow. This is unexpected. I feel a little twinge of worry. They dropped us off here to "free" us as a debt to Bek, Elly's mate. What if they've decided that human slaves are too valuable to send off to the ends of the galaxy and decided to retrieve us? I bite my lip at the thought and again have to resist the urge to clutch at Warrek's belt to steady myself. However icy it is here, and however much I feel out of my depth amongst all these hardy, capable people, it's better than being a slave.

I glance up at Warrek. "What is it doing here? I thought they weren't coming back? Ever? Do you know anything about this?"

But Warrek stares at the ship, then shakes his head slowly.

At least it's a response. Just...not a very reassuring one.

"Are they bringing more slaves?" I press. Maybe the people running the ship have decided to turn over a new leaf as good Samaritans and brought more humans to come hang out here? Even as the thought rolls through my head, though, I don't buy it. They were kind of an unfriendly crew. I doubt they'd do anything that didn't benefit them, and it was clear they didn't like slaves—or humans. Why bring more? I keep watching Warrek, hoping he has answers.

He gazes down at the big, dark ship in the valley and then slowly shakes his head again. Then, miracle of miracles, he speaks. "I...do not think they should be here."

Great. The only words he's said in two days are scary ones. I fight the gnawing fear in my stomach at the thought.

WARREK

The little human female's distracting chatter has quieted. I do not know if I like that she's gone silent or if it worries me. The endless stream of conversation she feels the need to expel like puffs of air has come to an end, and now I do not know what she is thinking. When her hand steals to my belt and she holds on to it, I feel a protective surge.

She is frightened.

As the only male here in the cave with her, it is my duty to reassure her. But unlike her, I cannot think of the right things to say. All the clever thoughts that move through my head in quiet moments are gone, and I can only stare blankly at the sky, then down at her. Suh-mer wants answers, and I have none. Nor am I good at reassuring a female. I have never had a mate, nor a pleasure-mate in my furs. I do not know how to rid her of the worry in her gaze. I know how to fish, how to hunt, how to skin. I do not know how to talk to a female.

But I must do something. So I place my hand atop her head, like I would a kit, and give her a pat. "All will be well."

She reacts as if I have hissed at her, jerking back and slapping my hand away. "What the fuck? I'm not a child, thank you very much! Don't give me one of your patronizing little pats on the head, you dweeb!"

I blink at her. I did not grasp half of what she just spat at me, but it is clear she is upset.

"Sheesh!" she exclaims, crossing her arms under her breasts, giving me another indignant look, and then storming down the path toward the valley. "You know what? Never mind. I don't need you to answer me. You can sit here by yourself and be quiet. I'm going to go see what's up."

I watch her as she marches down the icy slope, back stiff. Even as I stare in surprise, I can see her dark, smooth hair icing over. It is hot inside the fruit cave, and damp, and she is going to be frosted over within a matter of moments. She will need warm furs to clothe herself in, and a weapon, just to be safe. As I watch her walk, she slides on the pathway, her shoes skidding.

And new boots, I think. And perhaps a walking stick.

I head back inside the cave and grab things quickly—my spear, several fur wraps, and the pack of supplies I always keep ready and at hand. I race down after Suh-mer, who is just now getting to the bottom of the cliff, and she gives a startled little scream when I appear at her side.

"Why are you so damn quiet? It's not cool to sneak up on people, you know. In fact, it's frowned upon in most cultures, but I guess that doesn't matter to you, right? But god, you scared the life out of me." She clutches at her chest, shaking her head. Her hair is now stiff with ice and looks frosty. "Not that I suppose you're going to apologize, because that would involve opening your mouth and saying words, right? And heaven forbid you talk to someone like me. But I guess you think I have enough words for both of us, right?" She gives me an exasperated look.

Should I apologize? I did not mean to frighten her. But I also worry that talking about it will just encourage her to say more, when it is clear she is cold. Still, I should say something. I think, and the knot forms in my throat. My father would know what to say. He would laugh at my inability to speak to such a female... but he is gone these last few seasons.

So I say nothing, simply pull out one of the furs and wrap it around her shoulders. I will let my actions explain themselves.

Suh-mer looks startled as I do, and she starts to slap my hands away again when she realizes I am simply draping a cloak about her small human shoulders. "Thank you," she manages. "I guess I should have thought about that when I left, but I'm not used to going from a warm place to a cold one. This entire planet feels like one big meat locker, and you forget that there can be warm places here, though I guess I shouldn't, since it's obvious that there's a lot of geothermal activity, right? So it would stand to reason that the heat is going to vent somewhere." She adjusts the furs around her shoulders and gives a little shiver. "But I guess I am rambling."

Does she...want a response? "Yes," I manage. That seems appropriate.

Her strange, smooth human face scrunches up as if I have insulted her again. "I think I liked you better when you were silent," she mutters to herself and turns her back. "Are you coming to say hello to the ship with me?"

I am not leaving her, that is for certain. Not when she is more helpless than many of the kits in the tribe when it comes to taking care of herself out in the wild. I watch as her boots slip on the ice again, and wordlessly offer her my spear as a walking stick.

"No, thank you," she says. "I don't want to hunt. I'm going to go visit the others. Visit," she emphasizes, slowing the word down. Then she sighs. "I don't know why I just did that. You're not hard of hearing, you're just ignoring me. Or being silent like Elly. Either way, it just means I'm going to keep rambling like a crazy person." She shoots me another look, and this one is almost amused. "You've been warned."

I...am not entirely certain of what she warns me of. Of her speaking? I like her voice, even if I do not know what to say to her. That is one reason why I listen so much when I am around her. It encourages her to say more, and I like hearing it. "Thank you," I tell her.

That appears to be the wrong answer, as well. Suh-mer makes another frustrated noise and wraps the furs tighter around her, marching forward across the snow. I remain at her side, slowing my steps to match her smaller, angrier ones. Of all the new humans that have arrived, I understand Suh-mer the least. Shail is motherly and kind, like No-rah or old Sevvah. Buh-brukh is flirty and craves attention, like Asha. Kate reminds me of Leezh with her strength, but she is sweeter of personality, like Li-lah.

Ell-ee is quiet and skittish, like a wild creature. I even understand that.

But Suh-mer? Her, I do not understand. She is almost as tiny as Shail, but she looks wildly different. Shail's mane is bouncy and full of tight curls, and she keeps it cropped short to her head. Suh-mer has a thick, smooth mane like the sa-khui, dark black, but I brushed my fingers against it when I put the furs around her and found it was softer than a snow-cat's fur. Already I itch to touch it again. The humans all have wildly different features, but Suh-mer has a hide that is more golden than the florid pink and white that most of the humans are, and too light to be the lovely brown of Tee-fah-ni and Shail. She has a pointy little chin and fascinating hooded eyes framed with dark, dark lashes. Out of all the humans, I find her appearance the most pleasing. It is not that I do not understand, though.

It is that she talks.

A lot.

As a hunter—and now as a teacher of hunters—I must by necessity be quiet. Even the most foolish of game animals will be chased off by lips that cannot stay together. Suh-mer does not understand this. She talks. And talks. And talks.

But the things she says are fascinating. It is as if her mind cannot stop on one subject, so she must discuss all of them.

I actually do not mind it. Most assume that my silence is because I do not wish for company and often leave me alone. Suh-mer seems to chatter on in the hopes that my silence will break and a dam of words will pour forth. So she continues to talk at me, and I listen in fascination. I do not wish to interrupt because I want to see where her mind is going.

Unfortunately, I think my listening has caused her to assume that I do not like her. Even now, she marches ahead of me with her back stiff and her shoulders straight, as if offended. I bite back the sigh rising in my throat—no doubt it will be offensive, too—and keep pace with her.

We are a long ways off from the ship itself—probably several hours' walk, with Suh-mer's much smaller strides, and there are many ridges to cross before we enter the valley proper. We are at the top of one crest when I decide I should tell her to pace herself. I try to think of the right thing to say when I notice that the ship in the distance moves, just a little.

Alert, I put a hand on Suh-mer's shoulder.

"What is it?" She blinks up at me, trying to shrug off my grip. "If you think I can't walk in this, you're wrong. I mean, it's not my favorite, but a little snow never killed anyone—"

I put a finger to my lips, indicating quiet, and then gesture at the ship off on the horizon. When she goes silent, I take a few steps forward, watching. We are fairly high up here and able to see for a long distance. Even so, I cannot make out the faces of those that descend the ramp of the ship. A small cluster of people have emerged from the Elders' Cave, blue figures that move toward the ramp.

Someone comes down the ramp, and I see a flash of orange. Odd. I do not recall any of the strangers having orange hides. I thought they were blue like us.

An uneasy feeling uncurls in my gut. "Suh-mer, get behind me," I murmur. I put a protective hand in front of her, holding her back before she can continue on the path that will lead her down the cliff and into the valley.

"What? What do you mean?" But she doesn't push forward. She just looks up at me.

I cannot explain. Right now I am too busy watching what is unfolding in the valley, where the other ship has arrived in front of the Elders' Cave. Something is wrong. It feels...off. I was not here the last time that the ship arrived, so perhaps I am mistaken, but even from this vantage point, I do not like the stance of those that come down the ramp. It reminds me of...predators, and how they slink when they are waiting to pounce.

But perhaps Suh-mer's vulnerable presence has me thinking too protectively. She is not mate, she is not kit, but she is a female and vulnerable. I feel the urge to protect her. I step in front of her, shielding her smaller body with mine. Just in case.

"Warrek," she says with an annoyed sound in her voice. Her hand moves to my side, as if she can push me out of the way. "I can't see, you big doof. Why...." Her voice dies. "What are they doing?"

My throat goes dry as one of the newcomers from the ship raises something to his shoulder. As I watch, the others that have rushed out to greet him scatter. Something flashes, and one of the blue figures that had come out to greet him drops to the ground.

Suh-mer gasps. "They shot him! Who—who was that?" Her hand grips at my leathers. "Warrek, what's going on?"

I do not have these answers. I desperately wish I did. I watch in horror as another comes down the ramp of the ship, and yet another blue figure—one of our people—is felled. The others are scattering, only to fall to the ground as well.

Suh-mer makes a sound of horror and buries her face against my side. "I can't watch."

I know the feeling. I wish I could turn away. I do not, though. I must watch and learn everything I can of what is unfolding below. I wrap my arms around Suh-mer and put a hand to her mane, holding her close to comfort her. I can feel her body shake with silent weeping, but there are no tears left inside me.

I am empty inside as I watch my people slaughtered below. I count, instead. Three blue forms are on the ground. No, now four. A fifth one stands in front of the scattered females, and I see a flash of bright pink mane. That must be Buh-brukh standing behind him. They pause for a long moment, and I wait for them to be slaughtered, a cold pit in my stomach.

But they are not. The newcomers wave their long, pointed shoulder spears that shoot light, and then the small group goes up the ramp, disappearing into the ship. One of the others splits off and heads into the Elders' Cave and a moment later appears with Har-loh, who is heavily pregnant, and her small son. They guide them toward the ramp, but she falls to the ground next to one of the blue figures.

Rukh, then.

The captors make her get up and half-drag her into the ship. As I watch, another pair emerge—that makes four that I have seen, total—and drag the bodies of the fallen up the ramp. As they do, one suddenly jumps to life and begins attacking, and they shoot the light at him again until he slumps to the ground once more.

Not dead, then. My heart thuds heavily in my chest. Not dead.

"Captives," I murmur, and stroke Suh-mer's soft, soft mane as she weeps against my chest.

"W-what?" She looks up, lovely eyes wet with tears.

"They have taken them captive," I tell her. "They made the sa-khui drop to the ground, and when they began to drag them inside, one woke up and fought until they used the lights on him again."

"Used the lights...?" Her brow furrows. "Oh, you mean their guns. It flashes light."

I nod slowly. "I do not think they are dead. They gathered the females and brought them into the ship."

She sucks in a breath. "They're enslaving them. But why would the crew of the *Tranquil Lady* do that?"

I shake my head. "I do not think they were sa-khui peoples. Their skin was orange."

"Then something happened to the old crew," Suh-mer says, worry on her face. "They were blue like you, and they definitely said they weren't coming back."

"Somehow, hunters have taken their ship and followed their star-trail back here to us."

"They're not hunters. They're slavers," she says bitterly. After a moment, she reaches out and slaps at my chest with both hands, ineffectively.

I stare at her in surprise as she does—is she meant to be hurting me? I am twice her size and her slaps are no more than playful taps against my skin. "What are you doing?"

"Motherfucker, you haven't said a word in days and now you choose to be chatty? I'm *pissed* at you!"

I frown down at her. I know from the one Leezh that "fucker" means something about mating, and in an unpleasant way. But why would my mother be brought in? "My mother is long dead. I do not see why—"

"Argh!" She throws her hands up in the air. "Why am I stuck with the most impossible alien ever? Forget all that, Warrek. Just tell me what we're going to *do* to rescue the others!"

2

SUMMER

*O*kay, so calling Warrek "motherfucker" was not my proudest moment. He's not, really. Well, at least, I'm pretty sure none of the sa-khui tribe have anything to do with their moms. And I don't normally have a salty mouth like Liz or Maddie or even Brooke. I'm just so frustrated and scared...and I took it out on him.

Now I'm staring at him, shoulders heaving, mind racing, and I'm ashamed that I lashed out. The apology I want to give is sticking in my throat, because I know it'll turn into a long, rambling explanation of why I called him that and probably why I decided to use a cuss word, and then I'll launch into etymology, and we don't have time for that shit. So, for once, I shut my mouth.

Warrek doesn't get pissed, though. He just gives me another one of those thoughtful, uncomprehending looks and then puts a hand on my back. "We are not rescuing anyone yet. We are going back to the fruit cave to wait for nightfall."

Wait, what? I stare up at him like he's crazy. Maybe he is. Maybe seeing what happened below snapped his mind. "We can't wait for nightfall! That ship's going to take off with our people inside it!"

"If it does," he says slowly, calmly, "there is nothing that you or I can do about it. If we march down there in the bright daylight, they will greet us with their light-spears and take us as slaves with the others."

I close my gaping mouth, because he's...not wrong. We can't just waltz up to them, indignant, and demand that they let the others go. Still, the thought of leaving them behind feels like...the worst possible thing to do. Like I'm the biggest, most selfish jerk in the world for even thinking it. "We really have to leave?" I ask, my voice dropping to a whisper at the thought. It hurts me physically just to imagine turning and walking away.

I know what it's like to be enslaved. I know that terror all too well. My hell started when I woke up to hear my college roommate screaming in the middle of the night. I sat up in bed and looked over to find someone—an alien someone with green skin, a thin body, and big eyes—standing over her bed. I gasped, and their attention turned to me. After that, all I remember is a flash of light and waking up in a dirty cell on a spaceship, my clothing gone. My roommate was nowhere to be found—I don't even know if she's still alive, and I guess I'll never know.

I was in a cell with Brooke, and we were waiting to be bought. It seems that humans are grabbed and sold on the black market like...gosh, I don't know. Like Chihuahuas. Except I think the people buying humans want them for far more nefarious reasons than people want a pet dog. I expected the worst.

I got dumped on the ice planet instead.

And, okay, it's not so bad here. The people are nice, and even if the weather sucks, it beats being in a slave hold. Anything does. I shudder, remembering the filthy straw in the small cell I shared with Brooke, the stink of our unwashed bodies, the buyers that would come in and give us lascivious looks, feeling our arms or hair, and one even looked at my teeth. It was horrible.

I can't imagine what Brooke must be thinking right now. She must be frantic at the thought of being enslaved again. And poor, pregnant Harlow with a mate and a young son—what's going to happen to them?

I stare up at Warrek, but he only reaches out and pulls the furs tighter around my body then gestures back at the way we came.

I know he's right. I know that he's not saying we're giving up. We're retreating to figure out a course of action. But I can't help but feel a little hysterical at the thought. I manage to hold it together—all of it—inside me as we head back to the cave. I'm silent. I'm actually proud of how quiet I am.

And then the wave of hot, moist air hits my face, and it feels safe again.

And I lose my cool.

A hysterical, noisy sob breaks out of my throat, and I drop to the cave floor.

WARREK

Suh-mer is weeping so hard that I worry she will make herself sick.

I know how she feels. My spirit feels lower than it ever has, perhaps even lower than when the cavern collapsed and my elderly father did not make it out alive. Somewhere out there, our tribesmates have been stolen and we are the only ones left...

Except for the village. Croatoan. If the slavers go there... I swallow hard at the thought. I do not like to think about that.

I feel helpless. Like Suh-mer, I want nothing more than to rush out there with my spear and demand that our tribesmates be freed. But I know that my job is to keep Suh-mer safe here at my side. That is what my chief would want. It does not sit well with me, but I cannot risk her. She is a life-bearer, and our tribe is still too small to risk one such as her.

The human's frantic sobbing slows to a few hiccups, and I look over to where she is crumpled on the floor, a huddled ball of misery. I want to wrap my arms around her and hold her close, but I remember her angry slaps and know I would not be welcomed. She blames me for taking her away when she would go to their side. Brave but unwise.

I feel hollow inside at the thought, but I know we must hide away and not be seen. I sit at the edge of one of the ledges and stare down at the lush greenery

Suh-mer sits up and flings her shiny hair back. She wipes her fingers under her eyes and takes a deep breath. "Okay. Okay. Okay." She hiccups and then nods and gets to her feet.

"Where are you going?"

"It's been at least an hour," she says in a tear-scratched voice. She heads for the entrance to the fruit cave. "I want to make sure that ship is still here."

I follow her, because I feel as if I must protect her, at all costs. We...might be the only ones left at some point.

I push the thought out of my mind. I am not going to think like that.

Suh-mer nods and heads back into the cave before I can make it to her side. "Still there." She scrubs a hand under her nose and sniffs. "I got my freakout out of my system. Now we need a plan to figure out how to save the others."

I watch her, amazed. Her voice is calm, and she takes deep, steadying breaths. "Rescue?" She is very brave—brave but foolish. "I am but one hunter, and you have never carried a spear. How will we rescue them against an Elders' Cave full of light-spears?"

"Don't you want to save them?" She moves to sit down on the slick floor of the cave, across from me.

"More than anything." My tribe is all I have after the death of my father. I feel responsible that they were taken while I was in the cave with Suh-mer, admiring her hair and the golden cast of her skin.

"All right, then, we need to think strategy." She blinks a few times and then grabs a small, chalky rock and begins to draw a grid on the stone floor. "I'm going to think of this like a chessboard. We're one player, and they're the opponent." She draws a circle outside of the grid. "That's them." She draws two small circles on the far end of the grid. "This is us. Now, we just need to think of this like chess. In chess, whoever's in control is the winner."

"Chess?" I echo. "What is this?"

"It's a game humans play," she says, coloring in some of the squares in her grid. There's an intent, focused look on her face. "You use strategy to outsmart your opponent. You're only allowed to make one move at a time, but if you do things wisely, you can control the game before your enemy even gets started. That's what we need to do here. We need to outthink them."

"In...this chess, you use light-spears?"

She shakes her head and starts to place berries on the grid she has created. "You have playing pieces and you move them. It's not a physical game. It's a game played with the mind. I'm pretty good at it." She gives me a small smile. "Chess club, you know? Didn't exactly make me popular, but I liked it anyhow. Now, these pink berries are going to be our pieces, and these darker, yucky-looking berries are going to be the others. Not that we really need berries or we need to map out our moves, but visualizing it helps me think things through. And talking. Talking helps."

"Then talk," I say to her. I like to hear her thoughts, anyhow.

She flashes me a quick, grateful look and then continues. "In chess, it's a mind game as much as it is a game of moves. You need to establish your territory before your opponent can, and once you do, you can keep them guessing and keep them off-guard as you strategize around them. These four squares here," she says, pointing at the center of her grid, "are the sweet spot. You control this, and you control the entire board. I'm going to think of this as the valley itself. Whoever controls the valley is going to end up winning this game between us and them. So..." She thinks for a moment and then continues, toying with one of the berries that threatens to roll away. "We're going to have to assume that they're not going to fly off in the next few hours. If they do, it doesn't matter what we do anyhow. The others will be lost to us no matter what we strategize." For a moment, her lower lip quivers, but she shakes it off. "It'll do no good thinking like that, so we just won't. I have to go with the assumption that there's a reason they're still here. Maybe they're staying for the night. Maybe they're recharging their batteries. Maybe they're waiting for more of the tribe to show up to nab them all. Whatever it is, they're still here, so we're going to use that to our advantage." She studies the board for a moment. "We need to make the first move."

I am impressed with her clever, quick mind. "Go on."

"In chess," Suh-mer says, picking up one of the berries and moving it forward. "The pieces have different names and different moves they can do. Normally I'd say we open with moving a pawn to create a path for the stronger pieces. Right now, though, we only have two pieces, so I'm going to sweep all of these others off the board and assume we're playing with a handicap." She pushes the pink berries aside except for two.

Interesting. "I saw four of them," I tell her, leaning forward and nudging some of the darker berries off of the "opponent" side.

She flashes me a happy smile, pleased that I'm following her strategy. "Okay, there might be more of them in the ship, but I don't recall it being that big. Unless they're all squished in the cargo hold, we're going to assume there aren't many more on there. Maybe the old crew." She thinks for a minute and then shakes her head. "No, two things must have happened. Either the ship got taken over and the crew was disposed of, or they're working together somehow. They took out Mardok like the others, you said?" At my nod, she continues on. "So we have to assume that they're not his friends. Let's go with four for now, and we can adjust them. And we're going to add another piece because they have the ship and we don't." She gazes down at the modified board, and I can see the thoughts racing in her head.

"And..." I ask.

"I'm thinking," she says, crossing her arms and tapping a finger on an elbow. "We're in a dangerous position right now. We've got two pieces, you and me. I'm counting you as the king, because just like in chess, if you get captured, I'm totally lost. I need you to win this. So that leaves me as the queen. She's the one that makes the big moves. But...I can't approach the ship. I wouldn't know what to do with it. I think my chess analogy is running out of steam." She picks up one of the pink berries and gives it a frustrated, miserable look.

I take it from her fingers and place it back on the board again. "If you were at home on your planet, and you wanted to stop someone from leaving, how would you do so?"

She tilts her head back and forth, thinking. "I'd take their car keys, of course. Can't drive the car, can't leave. But they have a spaceship. Then again, I suppose a spaceship can be like a car. I can't get the keys, though..." Her eyes brighten.

She has an idea. I gesture for her to continue. "Go on."

A smile spreads across her face. "Well...if we don't care about damaging the ship, we could always slash their tires."

3

SUMMER

*T*his is all on me.

I'm trying not to panic at the thought, but it's difficult. We have to rescue the others, and Warrek's letting me lead the charge. I can't fail. The thought's utterly terrifying, and I hope his confidence in me isn't misplaced. But as a sa-khui hunter, Warrek is out of his league when it comes to anything technological or relating to the ship. I'm the one that has to think outside the box. I just don't want to fail.

Warrek and I waited all afternoon long for it to grow dark outside. We took stock of our supplies. I'm surprised at how well-stocked Warrek is for a day trip. I thought we'd be screwed, but it turns out he keeps a survival bag with him at all times. He's got a spear and two knives, extra leathers and waterskins, fishing hooks and twine, a braided rope, and soapberries. Some of it isn't all that useful, but I'm glad we have it, just in case.

I'm nervous all afternoon, stealing out of the entrance to the cave to watch the ship in the distance. Part of me is terrified it's going to take off at any moment and Harlow, Farli and the others will be gone forever. But it doesn't. It just sits there on the horizon like a malignant tumor on the smooth surface of the snow. So at least there's that. It means that our plan for tonight can go ahead as we hoped.

Plan. Hah.

I have no plan, other than "somehow stall the ship." I've been racking my brain all afternoon, thinking up all the ways we could possibly prevent the ship from taking off. Tying down one of the "feet"—the landing gear—doesn't seem like it would work, since the ship can hover and land vertically with no need for a ramp-up. There aren't tires, so my metaphor for "slashing them" remains just wishful thinking. I can't see a tailpipe, so I don't know if we can stuff it and cause the engine to stall. If we were at home, I'd unscrew the gas cap or put sugar in the tank or any number of things I've heard will stall a car. Or heck, just pop the hood and unhook the battery.

But this is a spaceship, built by people with technology leagues and leagues ahead of ours. There might be zero vulnerabilities to us, in which case, my grand plans will fail. God, I really hope we don't fail.

Right now, we have a two-part plan.

Step one: stall the ship and prevent it from taking off.

Step two: flush out the slavers inside the ship and pick them off one by one. To do so, Warrek's going to dig pit traps and cover them stealthily, and we're going to take it from there.

I'm in charge of step one.

I have no idea what to do for step one. But I'm not going to let that stop me. We need a plan, and even a terrible one is still better than no plan.

As we head across the crunching snow into the night, though, I'm starting to get really, really nervous. What if we can't figure out how to stop the ship from flying off? What if I let everyone down? And because I get nervous, I start to babble. "I feel like we should set expectations before we get to the bad guys. Because I know what I'm capable of, but I'm not sure if you're aware of what I am and am not capable of, and I feel like if you think I'm capable of something and I'm not, then you'll be disappointed in my lack of capability, and then you'll feel like you're doing this alone. Not that you're doing it alone, of course. Or that I even want you to! I want to help as much as the next person. Oh man, I really wish there was a next person that could help." I mentally cringe. "Not that you aren't great, of course. I'm glad you're here and I'm not alone, it's just that—"

"I know," Warrek says quietly, and puts a hand on my shoulder as we walk. "You worry. I do, too. We will do what we can."

Not the most comforting of words, and yet it's exactly what I needed to hear. I suck in a deep breath. "Right. We've got this."

"You are clever, Suh-mer. You will know what to do." He gives me an intense look of confidence that makes my skin prickle. No one has ever looked at me like that.

"Okay."

"Just remember to be careful. We must not be seen."

I won't forget. The thought of being noticed by the slavers has me utterly terrified. I nod repeatedly, as if nodding more than once can somehow convince me, too.

And then we've crossed most of the valley and the ship looms a short distance away, so close that I can hear the gentle hum of the engines. Oh god, I'm so not ready. I swallow hard and look over at Warrek.

He pulls one of his bone knives from his belt and hands it to me. "I will begin digging the pit traps. Be careful."

Right. He's going to do the hard stuff and I'm going to scout things out. We can do this. I just need to stay cool and calm. "Okay." When he turns away, I reach out and grab his hand. It's startlingly warm, but not half as warm as the gaze he levels at me. "You— you won't leave me behind, will you?"

"Never."

Maybe he's just being polite, but that one soft word makes me think of all kinds of wholly inappropriate things. I feel my cheeks heating, and I start to nod again like a dummy, then catch myself.

Time to get things rolling.

Warrek jabs the end of his spear into the snow, looking for a slushy spot, and then drops to his knees and begins to dig with both hands, scooping snow with an inhuman amount of speed. I watch his bare blue forearms flex in the moonlight, then shake myself. No time to gawk. There's rescuing to be done. I clutch the knife close and head as silently as I can toward the big spaceship.

The goal is to get them out of the ship, I remind myself. While the enemy's inside the ship, they have defense systems I can't even imagine. Right now, they have control of the board. I need to get them into my territory and then slowly retake the spaces that they've claimed as theirs. It's doable in chess, with some smart maneuvering. It's going to have to be doable here, too.

I move closer to the ship and then hunker down in the snow near a boulder when I get closer, wondering if something is going to trigger a proximity alarm of some kind. I'm trying to think of every possible scenario, but when nothing happens, I have to keep getting closer. I wish I'd listened to Mardok when he'd told us about the ship, but I have to admit, I was more interested in watching the dreamy looks that Farli was giving her mate than what he was actually saying. He said something about it being a shipping cruiser. I remember that much. Okay, so if it's not a war vessel, it would stand to reason that it wouldn't make me explode into dust if I touched it, right?

Here's hoping.

I creep forward, then place one of my mittens on the hull. Nothing happens. I can feel the ship humming with energy, and the low sonic drone is much louder here. I look up, to the undersides of the wings, but everything is out of reach of someone my height. Right now I'm looking for a tailpipe of some kind. If I find one of those, I'm pretty confident I can find a way to jam it, and that always causes problems with a vehicle, I think.

I glance up at the wings again. I sure hope a tailpipe of some kind isn't under there. If it is, that's not going to happen unless I pull Warrek away. I glance back at him, but I can't see him in the dark. I picture him digging frantically because he's got at least two traps to create. I can't let him down.

I circle toward what looks like the back of the ship, and then I feel like smacking myself in the head. Near the end of the ship, tucked behind the wings and along the back of the body, there are a few pipes letting out a constant stream of exhaust. It's clear that they're hot, because they've melted all the snow in a wide circle on this side of the ship. "Summer, you doofus," I whisper to myself. "Look for the obvious clues first."

I approach, and as I do, I'm hit by a blast of hot air. I immediately take a few cautious steps backward and hunch low, trying to figure this out. Okay, I can't even get close to the tailpipes without turning into a charcoal briquette. I'll roast alive if I even try. I didn't consider that. I guess it's a lot easier on Earth to put a potato in someone's tailpipe when the car's not on. This car's on and it's not turning off.

Well, shit.

I slowly circle the ship again, giving it a wide berth so as not to set off any sensor alarms, and don't come up with any other ideas. Crap. If we're going to save the others, it's going to have to be with the tailpipe, unless I want to somehow go into the ship Rambo-style, armed with nothing but my knife, and try to do a takedown.

So...yeah. Tailpipe it is.

I circle around again to the back of the ship, noticing that I must have spent more time than I realized studying things. Warrek's smoothing out the small mountain of snow he's dug up from the one pit, trying to make it seem like a natural part of the environment. I know the plan is to grab a few rocks and weights to hold one of the furs entirely over the pit and cover it with a fine layer of snow so it looks completely disguised when you walk up to it. He says he's done it plenty of times before, so I'm going to assume he's got it covered. He sure doesn't look worried.

Me, I'm starting to worry I won't be able to handle my end of things. I return to the tailpipe and get as close as I can to the blasting heat, thinking. I'm about six feet away from the platter-sized hole that the exhaust is pouring out of. I need something sturdy to plug it. Of course, once I plug it, I need to make sure that whatever I shove in there won't immediately catch on fire, won't shoot right back out, and won't melt.

"Oh sure, Summer, no problem there," I tell myself sarcastically. "Maybe you can stuff it with the unicorn that's about to trot up, or ask a leprechaun to shove his pot of gold there. Both seem about as likely as you finding a solution."

But talking aloud helps me think, and I start stripping off the many layers of leathers I've got over my clothing. Each layer itself is too light to be useful, but maybe if I stick something heavy in the center—say, a rock—and then wrap it in heavier, wet leathers, the weight from those might stop it from shooting right back out. If I can make the ball of leather big enough that it'll expand when it dries...well, I actually have no idea if leather expands when it dries. But my hair fluffs when it dries, and my outer leathers are covered in a layer of furs, so it stands to reason that it'll do a little bit of puffing up, at least.

Then, maybe I can use Warrek's spear to jam the damn thing in long enough to cause it to backfire. If this is anything like my hairdryer at home—and gosh, it sure feels like it—blocking the exhaust will either cause things to shut off or something to catch on fire.

Either should bring someone out.

I have to be sure that our pit traps are ready at that point, though. It'll do us no good if we try to pull someone out and we don't have any place to trap them.

I get to work making my leather ball o' doom.

Finding a rock the size of a basketball isn't too hard. Finding one I can lift quickly means I have to size down to about a cantaloupe, though. I tear one of my layers of leathers into strips and begin tying the other layers over them. "Think of it like a big rubber-band ball," I tell myself. "With fur. And leather. And you're going to somehow get this magically wet."

I shiver at the thought of that, because it's bitterly cold out here. Without my insulating layers of furs, my teeth are starting to chatter and my skin is pricking at the chill in the night air. If this is anything like the Antarctic, it's probably a jillion degrees below zero at the moment. I don't know how much my cootie can handle, and my fingers are going numb, but I can't dwell on that now. What's a little frostbite compared to slavery?

I run out of leather and do a quick eye-balling of things. Nope, I need more. I find Warrek—who's digging a new pit in the distance—and am a little fascinated to see that he's stripped down to nothing but a loincloth to work. His skin is all shiny with sweat, and his long, silky hair is sticking to his back. Oh wow. That's...I give my head a little shake. "No distractions, Summer."

"Eh?" Warrek pauses, straightening and glancing over at me.

"Nothing! I just need your leathers. And your spear. But you're not using them, I see. Are you almost done? Because I don't know how long this will stay blocked, so we'll need to assume we have to hustle once I finish putting my pipe bomb together. Okay, it's not really a pipe bomb. It's a big wad of leather that's gonna go in a pipe, but hopefully it works like a bomb. Or really, I'd settle for it working like a plug. That would be fine with me—"

"Take my leathers," he says. "Give me..." He tilts his head and glances up at the sky, pointing. "Until the small moon crosses in front of the big moon. Then I will be done covering this pit. The other is already covered. Walk along the cliff," he says, pointing in the distance. "Do not come back this way or you risk falling in yourself."

I want to tell him that there's no chance of that, but...I am a klutz. There's every chance of that. I gather up his furs, snatch his waterskin and spear, and trot back to my workstation.

A short time later, my ball is done. Wetting it down turned out to be the easiest part, actually. All I had to do was load up the water-skin with snow, hold it close to the exhaust, and then pour the melted snow on top of the leathers. It's now damp—and rapidly freezing over—and heavy. I glance up at the moons—the little one's in front of the big one, and just about to exit.

Time to get this show on the road.

"Don't be nervous," I whisper to myself. "You're going to save everyone and be a big damn hero. That'll take care of any nervousness. You can throw up later. Right now, a big pool of vomit just means something else to slip in." I heft my heavy, slick weight into my arms. Holding it is a bit like torture because it's cold, wet, and getting my clothing damp, which means they're also immediately icing up in the chill. I glance around for Warrek, but I don't see him. Gotta do this myself.

I hold the ball out and try edging forward, but my hands start to burn. I pause to re-wet the ball, put my mittens on, and decide that the best tactic is to just rush forward and do things as fast as possible. The slower I go, the longer that super-heated air blasts on my skin.

"Count of three," I tell myself. "One. Two... *Three*." I rush forward, imagining myself making a basket in a basketball game. Be strong. Be fast. Be assertive. I ignore the blast of hot air and aim for the pipe. My plug goes in—and then doesn't go in very far. The air is powerfully strong and pushing against it hard. I jam at it with my fists, but the ball's getting too hot to touch. Fuck.

"The spear," I yelp to myself, and then wince when my voice seems far too loud without the roar of the exhaust. I don't have much time. I practically tackle the thing and then rush back, using the butt of the spear to shove the plug in farther with a few more jabs.

"Suh-mer?"

"Help me jam this in there," I pant at him. "Are you ready to go?"

"More than ready. We should leave the area." He moves to my side. "Now we go and wait—"

"First give this one good shove for me, okay?" I jam the spear butt against the rock-leather-ball thing again.

He gives it a few jabs, grunting, and then takes my hand. "We cannot stay."

"Right. Going."

To my surprise, he doesn't let go of my hand as we race away. We head a short distance away from the ship and huddle behind a pile of big rocks. I'm surprised we aren't heading back to the fruit cave, but I guess we want to wait and see if our traps spring any immediate results. Makes sense. I shiver, wrapping my arms around myself. Jesus, it's cold.

"Wait here," he murmurs, and gets up from our hiding spot.

I want to protest, until I see what he's doing. He grabs a fallen branch from a short distance away and uses it to sweep away our tracks in the snow, leaving only the ones that lead to the pit trap. Smart. He finishes and slowly continues to cover his trail, moving backward, his tail flicking back and forth high in the air as he walks his way back to me. Once he's behind the rocks again, he settles in next to me and then frowns.

"What?"

Warrek leans in and touches my face.

I jerk back, surprised. His fingers feel warm—and they also hurt. "Wh-what are you doing?"

"Your face is bright red," he murmurs. "And your eyebrows are gone."

"What?" I touch my face in horror. Sure enough, there's nothing but smooth skin where my eyebrows used to be. My eyelashes are gone, too. I can smell the singed hair now, and it hurts to touch my face. I pull my mittens off and my hands are bright red and tender, even through the leather. Oh god. "I...I was so focused on trying to push it in...I knew it was hot, but I didn't think..."

"You did what you felt you must," Warrek says softly. "It was very brave."

"I probably look awful," I whisper, grabbing a handful of snow and holding it to my cheeks.

"You look very brave."

I snort. "That's polite-speak for awful. You can tell me the truth, Warrek. Now's not the time to sugar-coat anything. Though I guess here it'd be snow-coat, since there's no sugar. Or if there is, you guys have been holding out on us. Not that I think you would, of course, but if it were me, and a bunch of strangers started to live in my city, I'd probably hide my valuables, too—"

"Your face is very appealing," he says in that low, calm voice. "Eyebrows do not change that. They only tell me that you are brave to risk yourself."

I feel that heat creeping through my body all over again at his words. Is he flattering me or just being nice? I study him, tongue-tied for a change, as he pulls his bag out and digs around in it. He pulls out a small little horn with a bit of leather tied on one end, and pulls off the leather. I realize it's a cap and there's a paste of some kind inside. "This will help your burns," he murmurs, taking my hand in his and beginning to rub the stinky lotion on the back. "Whatever this does not help, the khui will do the rest. You will be as lovely as ever in a few days, Suh-mer."

That definitely sounds like flattery to me. I practically squirm with pleasure at his words. It's totally inappropriate to be crushing on someone right now when others are in mortal danger. But as his fingers smooth the lotion over my hands, I start getting all jittery and flustered, and it feels like he's practically caressing some parts of my body that are a lot less safe than hands.

Or maybe that's just my hyperactive imagination.

I'm a little sad when he finishes covering my hands in the thin layer of goop. I want him to keep touching me. Of course, then he makes my heart flutter by digging a bit more of the lotion out of the horn container and gesturing at me. "Lean in."

Oh. Oh. He's going to touch my face. I don't know if my horny, inappropriate loins are going to be able to stand that. I should tell him no.

Instead, I practically shove my face forward so he can touch it.

Then I remember he's smearing some healing gunk on it and it's probably not a sexy look. This is not how dudes flirt to get women, Summer, I remind myself. Plus, you have zero eyebrows. Zero. I sigh at the thought.

"Hurts?" he asks in a low voice that makes my belly tingle.

"Just thinking," I whisper, all breathless.

His warm chuckle surprises me. "When are you not?" he asks.

I bite my lip as his fingers move over my forehead, smoothing the cool lotion on them. I'm still shivering with cold, but I can ignore that for now, considering that he's touching me—and he's sitting in a loincloth himself. It's not like we've got extra furs at the moment. They're all stuffed into the tailpipe, hopefully causing chaos. "I...I'm sorry if I tend to think out loud. I appreciate you being nice to me about it. I know it can be exhausting for people. It just helps me process to hear things aloud instead of in my head. Plus, I get nervous and start rattling off. I don't like long, quiet pauses. Um, like right now. I'm yapping because I don't like silence. Sorry. I'll shut up now."

But all he does is chuckle again and then begins to trace his fingers over my aching, too-warm cheeks. "Why be quiet?"

"Um, to give you a chance to speak? You're not exactly Mister Chattypants. And then because you're not talking, I feel the need to talk even more to try and find a subject to make you talk to me."

"Ah." He dabs at the lotion pot again and then smooths more on my other cheek. "I do not interrupt because I enjoy your conversation."

I'm shocked to hear this. "You do?"

He nods.

"You don't find it irritating?"

He shakes his head. "I am too quiet, I know. It has long been a habit of mine. But if it bothers you, I shall speak more."

"It's not that it bothers me, it's that I worry you don't like me."

Warrek pauses, wipes his hand on a small piece of leather, and then studies my face, head slightly tilted. He reaches for me again, and I close my eyes, obediently waiting for more lotion.

I'm surprised when his fingertips lightly brush over my lips, tickling me. "I like you," he says in a low, husky voice.

Oh mercy. Did I think my body was reacting before? I feel like everything inside of me just gave one giant, needy shiver.

Or maybe that's the frostbite.

I open my eyes and gaze up at him. He's not leaning too close to me, but his eyes are soft, his attention focused on me. His fingertips trace the curve of my mouth, and then he lightly continues along my jaw, tracing my skin as if learning me. It's the most erotic thing that's ever happened to me in my (admittedly sheltered) twenty-two years.

"Halloooo," a voice calls in the distance.

I gasp, my eyes going wide at the same time that Warrek stiffens.

4

WARREK

*T*he voice calling out is unfamiliar. I would recognize the sound of any of my tribesmates calling out in the space of a heartbeat...and this is not one of them. The inflection is strange.

Suh-mer grabs at my arm. "Who is that?"

"Enemy," I whisper, putting a finger to her lips to silence her. "He speaks the human language to trick us, I think."

She nods, eyes wide. Her fingers feel cold against my skin, and I realize that she is shivering. The nights are bitter for humans without coverings, and she has given hers up. I have nothing to offer except my loincloth, but it will do nothing to keep her warm. She needs to get back to the cave.

But how can I leave with her when we have just now lured one of the enemy out?

I hear a loud thump in the distance, and then something that sounds like Leezh when she is in a bad mood. Cursing always sounds the same, no matter the language. I peer over the rocks that shield us, and Suh-mer is at my side.

At the back of the ship, where Suh-mer put her strange leather ball, an orange stranger stands there, one of the light-spears in his hand. It is pointed at the sky as he glares down at a smoking mound. Suh-mer's leather plug. Her idea worked to bring someone out of the ship, and I am impressed even more by her clever mind. She touches my shoulder as the stranger moves. He sees the tracks in the snow. I watch, holding my breath, as he follows the tracks ever closer to our pit trap.

When the stranger lifts one arm and speaks into his wrist, I am confused.

"He's got a communicator on," Suh-mer says. "He's talking to someone back in the ship."

I grunt acknowledgment of her words, but I am worried. This brings a new angle to things. What if he falls into the pit and then tells the others not to come out to rescue him? It will be a problem. We need to remove it...or make sure that he is silent.

"If we can silence him," Suh-mer whispers, "Maybe the others will come out looking for him. We can pick them off one by one. But we've got to get him off that wrist-com."

Our minds are thinking alike. I nod. "Wait here."

I get up from our hiding spot and begin to creep along in the shadows. I pull my bone knife out and check to make sure that Suh-mer is staying safe behind the rocks. She is not behind me. Good. I will treat this like any other hunt, then. Even if the prey is down, that does not mean it is not dangerous. It only means I have the advantage. I must get his light-spear away from him and get the communicator off his wrist. This is just like any other hunting trip, I decide. The prey is just trickier. But I have never met a beast I cannot fell, and with Suh-mer waiting and hoping, with all of the others depending on me, I will not fail now.

I creep forward, placing each foot silently, slowly, in the snow. Speed is not the key here, but stealth. My prey is oblivious to my presence, his head down as he continues to follow the tracks left for him.

Then his arms fly up into the air. He disappears. A wet crunch and a thud echo in the valley.

Now is the time for me to act. I fly through the snow, covering the ground between us, racing forward. I must catch this enemy before he can think to act. There is no time.

I come across the pit and catch a glimpse of the stranger rolling around in the bottom. He clutches at his leg as if wounded. His light-spear is cast to the side.

Luck is with me.

I leap down into the pit and quickly toss the light-spear back out, onto the snow. I did not have time to make the pit as deep as I would have liked, and this stranger is almost as tall as me. He struggles to get to his feet, and I grab at the thick band on his shoulder and fling it out of the pit.

He growls at me and raises a hand, trying to strike me. He is strong, but I am, too, and I am used to dealing with wild animals and hunting game. He is no match for my skill.

I grapple with him for a moment and then manage to flip him onto his back. Even as he squirms, I pin an arm behind him, and then the other, and tie him like I would a dvisti carcass, limbs in the air.

"Warrek?" I hear Suh-mer's gasping voice overhead. "Are you okay?"

I look up, as I finish tying up my prisoner, to see Suh-mer with the light-spear in her hands. Her hair whips around her face in the cold night air, and she looks fierce—and scared—as she points the weapon at us. "I have him," I tell her.

She makes a sound of relief and then gives me a worried look. "What do we do with him now?"

The prisoner growls low, thrashing underneath me.

For a moment, I do not know what we should do with him. I cannot let him go, but I also cannot cut his throat like an animal. He is a person. I do not know what to think. My people do not attack others of our kind. Even though this one is a stranger, it feels wrong to take him out like a sick dvisti. "I...am not sure."

"Should we interrogate him?" she asks. "Bring him back to the cave and find out what he knows?"

Suh-mer's quick mind has saved me once more. She is wise. I nod and begin to tie a strip around the prisoner's eyes. "We will make sure he does not know where we are going."

SUMMER

I have to admit I'm constantly surprised by mild-seeming, quiet Warrek.

Not only was he an absolute beast when it came to subduing our captive, but he hauls him out of the pit and carries him over his shoulder in the snow as if he weighs nothing. It's a long walk back to the fruit cave, and by the time we manage to get inside, I'm exhausted. I can't imagine how Warrek feels, but instead of collapsing with fatigue, he sets the prisoner down, ties his feet, and then comes to my side. With one hand, he pushes me down onto a rock. "Sit. Give me your hands."

I blink at him in surprise, and when I don't immediately offer him my hands, he takes one in his and rubs it, warming it and examining my fingertips.

"The cold has bitten at them," he tells me with that quiet, even tone of his. "But your khui will be able to fix the damage, given a few days." He carefully folds my fingers to my palm, making a fist. "You must tell me if you are in pain, Suh-mer."

I stare at him, surprised. "My fingertips don't matter if we can't save the others—"

"They do if you are the only one left."

Just like that, I'm stunned into silence. I didn't think about that. What if...what if Warrek and I are the only ones left on the planet after this? The thought is terrifying and lonely...and oddly sexy. I don't want it to be sexy, though. I want the others around. I want the tribe. The thought of being alone with Warrek can be sexy without all that other garbage.

My mind is a mess, I think. It's stress causing me to fracture mentally. That must be it. I don't say anything as Warrek drapes one of the furs over my shoulders and tucks it around me, even though it's sweltering inside the fruit cave. I understand why he's fussing over me now. In his eyes, if we're not captured and the village is, we're the only ones left. That's a sick twist to things.

Warrek moves back to the prisoner, who is huddled against the vines. He squats low, his long, blue legs flexing and tail flicking as he sits near the orange-skinned alien. "Why are you here?"

The thing looks at him with black, fish-like eyes. It chokes out something that sounds rude and snaps needle-like teeth at him.

Warrek doesn't look flustered, though. He reaches out and thumps the alien on the brow with his finger. "*Why* are you here? Do not pretend you do not speak the human language. It suited you to speak it earlier."

The alien laughs at him. "Why am I here?" it asks, voice strange and words slurred together. "Why are *you* here?"

Warrek ignores the question. "Are you slavers? Is that why you have taken my friends?"

When the creature just continues to grin at Warrek, I take the laser gun and aim the end that looks like a barrel at the thing's head. "Maybe we practice using this thing on him. That might make him a little chattier. I'm sure I can figure it out with enough fiddling around."

The alien goes still, and I feel a surge of triumph. "What is it you wish to know?" he says, words mangled through his strange teeth. "We are slavers, yes."

"What happened to the old crew?" I ask, because I can't help but wonder. "Are they working with you?"

"The old crew?"

"Yes, where are they?"

He grins, and it looks like pure evil. "The blue ones? I imagine their bodies are floating somewhere near the asteroid belt."

I gasp.

"You killed them?" Warrek asks, his voice calm and even. "Why?"

"Our ship was flagged by the—" He says a word I don't understand. "We needed to escape. They were unlucky enough to cross our path." He tries to shrug his shoulders in the ropes. "Such is life at the edge of the galaxy."

"So you killed them and hijacked their ship?" I try to recall a kind face among the lot, but mostly I remember them being exasperated by the weepy, frightened humans. Still, they didn't deserve to die because they were jerks. No one deserves to die like that. I swallow hard. "Why come here, then?"

"It was logged in their records as a landing, but no reason given. My captain thought they were hiding something here. It turns out they were." The toothy grin he gives us is cold. "Humans fetch quite a bit if you know who to sell them to."

His hatefulness makes my gut churn. "Is that why you attacked the others? Are they alive?"

The evil, toothy smile just grows wider, and it frustrates me. I move forward and push the end of the gun against the side of his head, just like I've seen in the movies. I want to wipe that smile off his ugly face. "Are the others alive?" I repeat again.

"Of course they are alive," he spits out. "Slaves are no good to anyone dead."

I breathe a sigh of relief at that. They're alive. And if they're keeping them as slaves, they're going to keep them alive. All we need to do is somehow stop them from leaving this planet and we can fix this. I feel such intense relief that it staggers me. I need to sit down. I wobble over to the nearest rock and sit heavily. There's still a chance. We've got this.

"Why are you still here?" Warrek asks the alien.

This time, his laughter disappears. "Why would we not be here?"

"Um, because it's smarter to take off with the slaves you have than risk things? Or like, hover in orbit? Seems to me that parking your ship in hostile territory is the height of stupidity."

The alien just scowls at us, but he doesn't offer any more information.

Something about this is very weird. I give Warrek a curious look.

He gazes thoughtfully down at the orange alien. "What are you waiting for?"

But our captive is silent. There's something he obviously doesn't want to tell us. He shifts uneasily and avoids eye contact.

Something's wrong, then. "Is it because you can't leave? Is that it?" I keep thinking, my thoughts whirling faster and faster. Just because I hijack someone else's car doesn't mean I know all the ins and outs of driving it. If I'm used to driving an automatic and my new car's a stick, I can't go anywhere. I imagine it's worse for a boat or a plane... How many times worse is it for a spaceship? "There's something with the controls, isn't there?" I remember that ungainly wobble it made as it landed. "You guys can't figure out how to leave just yet."

"You don't know what you're talking about," he sneers.

I bet I do. If that's the case, it buys us a little time.

I sigh with relief, slumping forward.

Even as I do, the alien springs into action. He plunges forward, the ties on his wrists snapping, and his arms fly out. He lunges for me, and I fall backward with a shriek, landing near the edge of the cave lip. The fruit cave is like a big hollowed-out gourd in that it has a lot of layers along the sides and not much in the middle, and one wrong step means death.

"Suh-mer!" Warrek pushes forward and grabs the alien. The creature wrestles with him, and as I watch, the alien scrambles for the gun. Warrek jabs the thing in the throat with an elbow and then kicks him hard in the chest, sending him backward—

Right over one of the vine-covered cliffs.

I squeeze my eyes shut, and then there's a sickening thud far below. Oh god.

Hands touch me, caressing my burned face and smoothing over my hair. Warrek. "Suh-mer," he says in that low, intense voice of his. "Are you well?"

"I'm okay," I breathe, letting him help me to my feet. "Just shaken." Understatement of the year. I'm trembling all over. "He…"

"Got free," Warrek agrees, running a hand up and down my arm as if to make sure that it's not broken. Or to comfort me. I can't figure out which. "My fault."

"What? No. Not your fault." I shake my head, then lean in slightly closer, because for some reason, I want a hug. Maybe that's weird, but when Warrek obligingly puts his arms around me, I want nothing more than to burrow against his chest and forget about the world. I can't stop shaking. "I'll be fine in a minute," I tell him. "Promise. I'm just trying to get my heart to calm down. Adrenaline, you know. I've heard it happens a lot when you're in a fight-or-flight situation, and I guess this qualifies, right? Though there wasn't much fight, and the whole flight thing—"

"Hush," he murmurs, stroking my hair back from my face. "You are safe."

Yeah. I guess I am.

I press my face against his warm skin, eyes closed. "And is he—"

"Dead? Yes."

Should I be sad? I'm not. It's not like he was a good guy or that we could let him go. He was bad. A slaver. Evil. But someone just died…and I'm just shaken.

Warrek strokes my hair again, his hand moving over my hair and then down my back. "I have you."

His voice is low and soothing. His touch—and his voice—make me feel better, and slowly I stop feeling that frantic terror. It changes to something else, and I become acutely aware of his warm, soft, suede-like skin against mine. I want to run my fingers all over him and pet him, but I guess that's weird. He's so strong and yet so wonderful to touch. And he hugs me. Gosh, I have needed so many hugs lately.

It's like Warrek understands me. Really and truly understands what I need. It feels so...good. And I'm starting to get that excited little curl in the pit of my belly again. I think about when he touched my mouth, and I look up at him.

The expression on his face is thoughtful.

I can't stand it any longer. I grab a handful of his long, silky hair and go up on my tiptoes, pulling him down toward me. When he leans in, I press my mouth to his and kiss him. His mouth is just as I imagined it—soft and yet warm and firm underneath mine. His lips feel perfect.

He's also not responding. His body has gone stiff against me.

Oh crap.

I jerk away, releasing his hair. "I'm sorry. I'm sorry. I fucked things up, didn't I? Here we were being friends and I had to just push things too far. I always do that. Let's just blame it on the adrenaline, okay?" I give a nervous laugh, and before he can say anything, I continue. "Pretend that never happened. I mean, it was just a kiss. Didn't mean anything. It wasn't even a real kiss, either. There was no tongue involved. Not that I was going to add tongue, especially if you weren't into it. I'm just saying that in the future, if I kissed you, there'd definitely be a bonus. Not that my tongue is a bonus." God, I just keep blurting words and he just keeps staring at me with that unreadable look. "You know what? I think I need a breath of air." I turn and head for the entrance of the cave, desperate to get away.

God, why do I have to mess everything up? He's being polite and friendly, and I had to grab his hair—*grab his damn hair*—and force him to kiss me. Ugh, if I were a dude, I'd be such a creep. I kind of hate myself right now.

My face burns with shame as Warrek eventually comes outside and stands next to me. He's silent, but then again, he's silent a lot. I cross my arms over my chest and do my best to ignore the chilly air. "So. What do we do now?"

He doesn't respond right away, but gazes out on the moonlit snow. "We will have to bury the body. It will begin to stink right away. I will climb down and retrieve it."

I wrinkle my nose at the thought. "And then?"

He looks thoughtful. "Then I suppose we dig more pit traps and try to catch the others."

WARREK

She kissed me. Pressed her mouth to mine in the bizarre human custom that I have never understood.

Now I understand it.

And now I wish I had kissed her back.

5

WARREK

*T*he next evening, we set up near the pit trap. Suh-mer carries the light-spear — a gun, she calls it — and I have made a few more spears of my own. No one has come out of the ship to investigate, and our traps are as yet untouched.

But the ship has not moved from its spot in the snow. They do not seem to be leaving anytime soon. That is good.

Suh-mer has returned to rambling around me, her voice high as she chatters. She is nervous.

I should have pushed my mouth against hers in return. I should have suggested she give me her tongue like she mentioned. Perhaps I am not as aggressive as I should be. Bek would have claimed Ell-ee's mouth for his own, I think. Or Harrec. Even Vaza.

It is just...pursuing a female simply for pleasure is not something I have ever considered. I always thought that if something would happen, it would be with resonance. When there were no unmated sa-khui females, I assumed I was meant to be alone and leaned heavily on my father's company and teaching the young kits how to hunt to fill the loneliness.

I did not ever expect the other humans to arrive. And when I did not resonate to them, I was not surprised. But I also did not expect...Suh-mer. Suh-mer with her lovely mane and golden skin and her mouth that moves constantly with her worried thoughts. Suh-mer with her clever mind and the way she holds on to me when she is scared, as if I am her protector. It makes me want to *be* her protector.

It makes me wonder at the pleasures of sharing furs with a female, even if it is not meant to be forever. Perhaps I will never be chosen to resonate. Does that mean I am to spend my life alone? I think of Shail and Vaza, who are happy and flirt constantly. It does not matter to them that there will never be resonance. They have been enamored of each other from the beginning.

And what if we are unable to rescue the others and it is only Suh-mer and myself left here on this planet? How will we react to each other then?

These are not questions I have answers for. I know only that I think about her all night long, and I worry over the kiss I did not give her as much as I worry over the safety of the others.

Tonight, Suh-mer is heavily bundled in furs as we sit behind the shield of rocks near the pit trap. There is no snowfall, so our tracks are not covered. The pit trap has been reset. That is good. Now all we must do is wait. I am certain they will not leave without their crewmate, and they must be wondering what has happened to him. His armband has chirped and flashed repeatedly throughout the day, so they are aware he is missing.

They will come after him. And when they do, we will be ready.

But until then, there is a lot of waiting. Suh-mer sits next to me in the snow, her gaze focused on other things. She deliberately avoids looking in my direction, and the silence between us feels... awkward. Normally, I do not mind quiet, but with Suh-mer, I long to hear her thoughts.

So I am the one that breaks the silence between us. "If this was your game, what would your next move be?"

"My game?" She looks over at me, startled. "Oh, you mean chess?" Then she gets flustered and waves a hand in the air. "Of course you mean chess. I don't know why I even had to ask that. I guess that's just me being silly. Or obtuse. Or both. Or—"

"Chess," I agree, interrupting to focus her.

"Right." She chews on her lip, the light-spear balanced in her lap. "Well, we have control of the board for the moment, and we just took one of their pawns. At least, I'm going to assume it's nothing more than a pawn, because we don't know how many of them there are on the ship. There could be fifty. There could be five. That could be the only guy and we'll never know." She frowns to herself, then shakes her head. "I do think there's more than just one, though. Someone's beeping his communicator. So, okay. If we're playing chess and I just captured one of his pieces, what would I do?" She tilts her head and then nods slowly. "I'd try to keep my opponent off-guard. Plan a move he's not thinking of. Try to go on the attack if it's safe."

"And if it is not?" I glance over at the ship. It is still large and intimidating. We do not dare approach it in case they are aware that their friend is gone and have set their light-spears on us. Suh-mer told me earlier she worries over such a thing. They know something is happening. They will be alert and wary.

"Then I would wait to see what they would do." She gives me a little half-smile. "Which is what we're doing."

I nod. It is not the best answer, but it is a wise one. I want to keep her talking, though. I like the sound of her voice. It comforts me. Makes things seem not so difficult. "Did you have a pleasure-mate back on your home world?"

She looks startled at my question. Her mouth opens, and then she closes it again with a snap. "Pleasure-mate?" she eventually asks, the sound strangled. "I...no. I'm kind of invisible to men."

Invisible? My knowledge of their language tells me that this word means she is unseen and ignored. How is this so? She talks all the time. "How do they not see you? Is it because you are not very tall?"

"What? I...no. That's not it." She nervously tucks her mane behind her ear. "I am sure they see me just like they see any other person. I just meant that they don't look in my direction when it's time to find a mate. I think I'm unappealing to men, or they don't find me sexy."

Sexy. That is a human word for mating appeal. I study her—her delicate features, her attractive mane, and soft-looking skin. Her slight form and the swell of her teats against the layers of her tunic. Why would they not find one such as her appealing? I would take her as my pleasure-mate without a second thought. But I do not tell her this, because I do not wish to fluster her. So I grunt acknowledgment.

"What about you?" she asks. "How come you've never taken a mate?"

She asks about me? I feel a burst of pleasure at the realization. It makes me feel...special in her eyes, and I decide I like that feeling quite a bit. "Many reasons."

When I don't elaborate, she nudges me with her boot. "I've got all night, buddy. Give me a few reasons."

I chuckle. "Apologies. My habit is to not talk about myself."

"And I have the opposite problem. But we can meet somewhere in the middle. Tell me why you never had a mate."

I ponder this. "Well...lack of females is one reason. Growing up, the only two females in the tribe that were unmated were Asha and Maylak." I shrug. "Neither of them struck my interest, and there was no resonance. I did not see the need to fight with others for their attention."

"That's fair. But what about when the humans arrived?"

"That is...different. I did not resonate, and I suppose I was waiting for that."

She makes an exasperated sound. "But if you were interested in someone, you should have gone after them."

Suh-mer is not wrong. Though I was not interested in any of the humans, she is wise to chide me. "I admit to being...hesitant at chasing a female. My father was broken when his mate died. I was young and do not remember my mother very well, but I remember my father's grief. It took him many, many seasons to recover, and even then, he missed her every day for the rest of his existence."

"That's so sad," she whispers. "He's gone now, I take it? You speak of him in the past tense."

"He died in the cave-in a few seasons ago. Our home collapsed, and as we rushed to get out, I did not realize he was not behind me until...much later." I feel a stab of guilt and grief. Even after several seasons, I miss my father's easygoing presence. "He was old, but he had many good seasons in him yet."

"How old are you?" she asks. "I'm curious."

"Fifty-six seasons."

Suh-mer sputters. "You what?"

"Our kind is very long-lived."

"God, I guess so. You don't look like a silver fox to me." She leans in and tweaks a few strands of my hair. "No grays yet."

I smile. "I will not become gray for another fifty seasons I imagine."

"Then I guess in a sense, you're not that much older than me. At least, not enough for it to be weird." Her face colors bright red. "For our *friendship* to be weird, that is."

"Do your people not approve of friendships between different ages?" I ask, curious. I have not heard such a thing from the other humans.

She squints in the direction of the ship. "Oh look. Is that someone? No, I guess it's just my imagination. Do you suppose someone else is going to come out soon?"

I blink at the flurry of her skittish words. Sometimes her mind is difficult to follow. "It is my hope they come out soon, yes, but I am prepared to wait all night."

"Me too." She shifts on her rock and stares straight ahead.

It grows quiet between us again. This time I do not feel lonely, though. I am thoughtful. Suh-mer's words have given me much to think about. Perhaps I have been too complacent. Perhaps it is time to stop waiting for resonance to come for me and to choose the female I wish to spend my days with, like Vaza and Shail.

Perhaps like in her game of chess, I should take my opponent off-guard in order to win.

Not right now, though, I decide. Our focus needs to be on rescuing the others. But once they are safe, I will let Suh-mer know she is to be mine. Even if all of the humans were not mated, she would be the one I would choose. Her face, her form, and, most of all, her mind all appeal to me greatly.

I will wait for resonance no more.

SUMMER

Sometime close to dawn, another alien does in fact come out of the ship. It's another one of the orange creatures, and this time, when Warrek jumps down in the pit after him, the fight goes on longer than it should, and I begin to worry. I shoot the laser gun —and the alien slumps, dead.

I mean, that's one way to take out the enemy, but I can't feel good about it. I know the rules here are different, but I just killed a guy. It doesn't matter that he's a bad guy, I still feel guilty.

I cry over it, too, but just a little, and only when I think Warrek isn't looking. I don't want him to think I'm a wuss.

I mean, I am a wuss, I just don't want him to think it.

At this point, though, we have two guns. We strip the dead guy of anything that looks like a weapon or a communicator, pile snow over his body to hide it, and retreat to the fruit cave once more.

"Get some sleep," Warrek tells me. "I will keep watch over the ship to make sure it does not leave."

As if we could stop it even if it did decide to leave. But I nod at him and lie down with the furs, ignoring the steamy heat of the cave as best I can. Never thought I'd prefer my chilly little hut back in the canyon village, but after days and days of the sauna-like fruit cave, I'm starting to get tired of all the endless hot, wet damp.

My face feels better, though. I touch my fingertips—which also feel better—lightly to my skin, and wish that eyebrows and lashes returned as quickly as my new layer of skin did. It hasn't been important to me that I look as attractive as possible...until now, of course. I glance up at the entrance of the cave, but Warrek isn't looking in my direction.

In fact, he hasn't really paid much attention to me outside of chatting, and I just feel so awkward about that kiss. Thinking about it makes me want to curl up with shame. He's just being nice, and here I think it's interest and decide to smooch him. What if he's gay? He could totally be gay, and that would be fine. But now every time I look at him, I'm going to remember that I tried to hit on him and failed miserably.

And it's a small damn village.

Despite the turmoil in my head, I manage to doze off for a few hours. Warrek and I trade "watch duty," and he catches a bit of sleep. Then it's nearly night again, and time to decide our course of action for this day. I gaze out at the ship, and I notice that the ramp hasn't gone back up.

Either they're inviting us in...or something else is wrong. I know we saw four. At least four. That leaves two and some possible buddies unaccounted for. I don't like this.

I also don't like waiting, either. By now they're going to be aware they're being picked off.

"I don't know how much longer they're going to be here," I admit to Warrek as I point at the ramp that's still in place. "It feels like every hour is another hour that could risk the others. What if we wait too long and they figure out how to fly the ship?" I gesture at the laser gun in my lap. "We're both armed as well as they are now. Maybe it's time to take them off-guard and make our move on the board."

He nods. "You and I share similar thoughts. What is your suggestion?"

It's flattering to be asked my opinion, but I feel wholly inadequate to offer one. "I don't have a lot of experience with battle."

"Hunting is not much like this either, I am afraid." He almost sounds amused.

"No, I guess not." I blow out a long, anxious breath. "Okay, well, then I guess we head in under cover of night. We could wear the armbands to throw anyone off and make them think their friends are returning. If nothing else, the armbands might have a passcode of some kind. Other than that, we just head toward the ramp, charge in, and hope for the best." I wince to myself. "That sounds like a terrible plan, but I really don't know what else to do. We can't let them leave with the others."

"I agree," he says quietly. "Even if we risk our lives, it is a risk we must take."

I nod. "It sucks, but there's no other option. I know the others would do the same for us if the tables were turned. Plus, the village..."

He nods, his expression grim. "They cannot get to them. The kits must be kept safe at all costs."

"We are in total agreement. You know how to shoot your gun?"

"About as well as you."

"Well, that's not totally comforting, but I get what you are saying." I smile brightly at him to hide my nervousness. My stomach feels like a big ball of nerves, and even feasting on a ton of delicious fruit hasn't helped things much. "If there's no reason to wait, then we'd best start hiking. The suns are going down right now."

Warrek nods thoughtfully.

I turn away to go put on my wraps. The moment I do, he grabs my wrist and turns me back around to him.

"What—what is it?" I look up at him, breathless. Just that small touch on my wrist is enough to make my insides flutter.

He steps closer to me. He leans in, his long, silky hair fluttering as he does. Slowly, he brushes his knuckles over one of my cheeks and then presses his mouth to mine. "If we survive this night, I am claiming you as my pleasure-mate."

I gasp. "You—you what? You are?"

He nods. "You will show me this kiss with tongue, and I will take you to my furs and make you mine. I have decided."

"Decided?" I echo, stunned. I can still feel the light brush of his lips against mine.

"Yes. You are my opponent, and I am going to take control of your board."

That's the sexiest, most bizarre thing I've ever heard.

Now how am I supposed to concentrate?

6

SUMMER

*D*espite the chill of the night air on the ice planet, I'm a nervous, sweaty wreck as we approach the ship. I hold my gun close to my body with sweaty hands, and try to stay calm. I *fail*, but I try at least. I glance over at Warrek, who is creeping next to me in the snow. It seems impossible, but his footsteps make no sound on the ground, unlike my crunching ones. He's going to have to teach me how to do that sometime. He seems impossibly calm, too, like none of this rattles him.

Maybe I got all the nerves between the both of us.

A light flashes on my borrowed armband, and I pause. Warrek does, too, and we give each other uneasy looks.

"Should I push one of the buttons?" I whisper. We're both wearing the bands stolen from the bad guys. They're covered in a variety of small buttons with strange markings, and we've been careful not to activate anything, just in case.

Warrek studies his wrist. It's now blinking, too. He thinks for a moment, then shakes his head. "We should not warn them, but we will be cautious as we enter."

"Cautious. Right." I hold my gun a little tighter. "Because I totally am thinking 'cautious' as I go in and raid an alien ship. With a gun. Did I mention the gun? Because we already shot one dude and threw another off a cliff and I'm just thinking that—"

He puts a finger to my lips, silencing me—and reminding me of his promise for "later." I'm all flushed with anticipation at the thought, but then he points at the ship. Right. One thing at a time.

Rescue first, sexytimes later.

I nod to let him know I understand, and then we're creeping toward the ship once more. It looks ghostly and empty as it sits on the snow, and my big blob of leather is still in the bare spot by the tailpipe. I kind of wonder if we should try jamming it again, but what if it makes something in the ship explode and no one comes out? Then we're basically killing our friends. All of our choices are bad ones.

"You remember how to shoot?" I whisper to Warrek as we move toward the ramp. We practiced earlier, but even with all the practice I've had messing with the laser gun, I'm still scared I'm going to mess something up.

He nods and then gestures at the ramp. "I will go up first."

"You what?"

Warrek grins at me. "Did you wish to go up first, then?"

"Well, no! But—"

"Then I shall go." He glances at the lit ramp, which is disturbingly empty. "If I do not come back out or give you a signal after a hundred-count, do not come after me. Take yourself back to the fruit cave and stay there."

"What?"

He doesn't explain himself, though. He just raises his laser gun to his shoulder and immediately heads up the ramp.

I hold my breath, waiting.

There's a shout. A shot rings out. More yelling.

Fuck this. I'm standing here like a doofus, waiting in the hopes that Warrek—a barbarian—remembers how to shoot his gun? I can't. Everything in me rebels at the thought of standing around. I brace my long, unwieldy gun against my shoulder and head in after him.

The ramp itself looks deceptively peaceful, but as I go up, another shot rings out, and a laser sizzles overhead. Light shoots past, and I bite back my yelp of surprise. It wasn't aimed anywhere near me. "You've got this, Summer," I whisper to myself. "Fake it until you make it."

I take a few more steps forward, and then I see a flash of blue skin. It's Warrek, hiding in the shadows of what looks like a stack of strange plastic crates near the top of the ramp. He's pinned down, I realize, as another laser flies past. I follow the source of the laser, only to see another orange-skinned alien hiding a short distance away.

He sees me the same time I see him.

And that, of course, means that I'm completely visible. There's no room to hide next to Warrek where he's at, either.

Well, I'm going out shooting, then. I put my finger down on the button that activates the gun, and shoot.

Aim? Not so much. But I do shoot.

My blast goes wide, but the alien ducks his head and yells something out in a strange tongue. I charge forward, continuing to shoot as wildly—and quickly—as I can. I race forward, yelling and shooting, and it takes me a few seconds to realize that the alien isn't all that far away and I've somehow managed to run straight at him.

And now I'm on him. So what do I do again? I shoot. Right at his face. He falls to the ground in a spray of blood, and then I'm standing over his body.

I just killed another man. Another bad guy, I remind myself, though I still feel sick to my stomach at the thought. I'm going to have to process that some other time, though, because Warrek's at my side, a furious look on his face. "Suh-mer! What were you thinking?"

"I don't think I was doing much thinking," I tell him faintly. "Can we not argue about this right now?"

Someone yells off in the distance, and Warrek gives me a frustrated glance. "You are not safe—"

"Newsflash, neither are you," I tell him. "I'm upset I just offed another guy, but let's get angry about that later, okay? Right now we still need to rescue our friends."

He nods and then pulls me closer to the wall, shielding me with his body as another man rushes forward. This time, he raises his gun and almost takes out Warrek before the big barbarian shoots him, and I experience a pang of fear and a little queasiness. Why is this so easy? Are guns really the answer? You can kill someone with the pull of a trigger...it seems unfair. I hate them, and yet I'm glad we have some so we can rescue the others. After this is done, though, I'm never killing another thing. Ever.

There's a long tense moment of quiet.

"Anyone else coming?" I whisper against Warrek's back. Now is not the time to notice how corded his muscles are or the fact that his tail is twitching against my front and tickling me. I need to pay attention to my surroundings—well, what I can see of them from around his side.

"I do not see anyone."

I nod to myself and put a hand on his waist, pushing him over slightly so I can scan our surroundings. We're in what looks like a cargo area—I guess, though I'm not that familiar with spaceships myself—and there are rows and rows of long, dark crates propped along the wall. Off to one side, there's a hallway, and on the opposite side of the room, another. "Okay, if the coast is clear, then we should probably split up."

"No," Warrek says, a stubborn note in his normally mild voice. "I will not put you in danger."

"That's cute and all, but you don't own me," I tell him with a little pat to his arm. "And you can yell at me later when the others are safe. For now, let's just get this stuff taken care of, okay? There are two hallways," I tell him, pointing at them. "You should take one and I can take one. The sooner we get this done, the sooner we're safe. All of us."

He sets his jaw, but nods. He doesn't like it, but he knows I'm right. When another voice yells out, he nods at me. "It sounds as if it is coming from there. I will take that one."

"Be careful," I tell him.

"And you." Then he shoulders his gun and he's gone, moving down toward the enemy with super-quiet steps. Damn. I'm really going to have to have him teach me that.

I watch him go and then give myself a little shake. Time to get moving. I race toward the other corridor, heart pounding as I hear laser guns go off in the other direction. I need to get my shit together and stay focused. I can't go chasing him. I have to trust that he's okay.

The hallway I head down has a few doorways, and all of the doors are closed. I pound on the entry-pad of the first one, because I don't remember how the old crew that rescued us opened the doors when we were first brought on the ship, weeks ago. It's been far too long and I wasn't paying attention.

Nothing happens, and I put my ear to the door to see if I can hear anyone moving inside. It's silent, so I move on to the next door. This one opens up to the med bay, but the room is empty. The supplies are scattered all over the floor, and the big long table is cracked. There's a dried stain on the floor that looks a lot like blood, but it also looks really old. Ugh. I do a quick sweep of the room just to be on the safe side and then head back out.

Two doors later, I find the cockpit.

Or at least, it looks like the cockpit. Or the bridge. Or whatever they call it in space movies. There are several chairs and stations set up—all of them empty—and screens display running numbers and foreign characters I can't make out. One of them is busted and gone dark, and I wonder if the old crew gave them a good fight. I sure hope so. I move around the room, but there's no one anywhere. It's just beeping panels and flashing switches and one station that looks like it could be controls for the ship.

Which gives me an idea.

I heft my gun and aim at the terminal. If I trash this, no one's leaving the planet. Granted, that means that me and the other humans would be stuck here forever...but we kind of thought that anyhow. This way, everyone stays for good—bad guys included. "I'm sorry in advance," I whisper to no one in particular and hold down the button to fire my gun.

Shooting up the panels makes a lot of noise and smoke, and sparks fly as the gun toasts everything I aim it at. The lights at each station go dark, the screens overhead blip out, and the terminals start to look more like melted slag than anything else. A light flashes overhead—probably an alert of some kind.

"What are you doing?" growls an unfamiliar voice behind me. "Drop your weapon!"

I immediately drop it, and then I mentally kick myself. I should have turned around and shot. Shit, why am I such an idiot? I inwardly wince and put my hands in the air.

"Turn slowly," the alien growls in English.

I do, and as I turn I see it's another orange guy. They're the ugliest things I've ever seen. From the rough pebbly skin to the overlarge head and the bulging eyes, it's a hideous creature. He's not going to be happy we killed his buddies, I bet. He stands in the doorway to the bridge area. I'm cornered, and there's nowhere else to turn.

"Hands higher," he snarls.

"I'm putting them up, I promise. Just don't shoot me, okay? I really appreciate living. And breathing." Oh god, my nervous babble is kicking in. "Though I suppose breathing comes with living, right? There's not a lot of breathing dead people. Though there is a thing where corpses do seem like they're breathing because of built-up gas in the lungs. I saw that on a documentary once. It turns out—"

"Shut up," he tells me. He pushes the gun barrel toward me, just slightly. "How many are with you?"

I hesitate, and when he shoves the gun near me again, offer, "Um, I thought you wanted me to shut up? I mean, I can talk if you want me to." A shadow moves behind him. I force myself to stay focused and not look at the person creeping up behind my captor, because I see a flash of blue skin and can guess who that is. "I'm also pretty good at singing and dancing, which might be a bonus if you're looking for entertainment slaves. I mean, not that I want to be a slave, but I'm guessing that's what you're wanting us for, right? So I might as well list my assets—"

"How many of you?" he snarls again, furious.

"Um, human or sa-khui? That's the blue guys. Because there's a different number of both, and I assume you'd want me to clarify. Do you want to know how many humans?" I wiggle a finger, still careful to keep my hands in the air. "Because there's me, and Harlow, and Kate, and Gail, but I'm guessing you already know about those ladies because you captured them, right? Oh, and Brooke. She's the one with the pink hair. It's not naturally pink, and she's going to have some pretty fierce roots soon, but I suppose that it doesn't really matter—"

"How many are attacking the ship?" he grits out, and steps closer to me, the gun rising higher. "Quit stalling and tell me what I want to know."

I swallow hard, because staring at the end of that barrel reminds me rather uncomfortably just how easy it is to fire a gun and blast someone's head off. "Coming on the ship right now?" My voice goes squeaky high. "Well, there's me and..."

"Me," Warrek says behind him.

There's a loud blast, and I duck my head as a gun goes off.

For a long, breathless moment, I think I've been shot. Then I realize I'm fine and nothing hurts. There's a heavy sound as the alien drops to the ground, and I squeeze an eye open. Warrek stands there, a fierce expression on his face as he kicks the alien aside and then pushes toward me. "Suh-mer. Are you safe?"

I nod silently. I think I used up all my words blabbering at the guard.

"Speak." He cups my chin in his hands. "I will not know you are well until I hear your voice."

I swallow hard. "I found the bridge." I tilt my head, gesturing at the destroyed panels behind me. "And I trashed it so no one else can leave."

"No one else is leaving," Warrek says in a strong, sure voice. "It is done. The enemy is defeated."

7

WARREK

*E*veryone is dealing with the stress of captivity in different ways, I realize as we regroup with the others. Some are quiet, like Shail. Her expression is hard and wary, as if she expects this all to be taken away again. Vaza hovers over her, comforting as best he can, but it is clear that Shail is acting remote and he does not know what to do.

Others are easier. Kate sobs, clutching her tiny snow-cat. "I can't believe they declawed him," she weeps as Harrec holds her close. "Monsters. How's he supposed to defend himself now?"

Harrec just strokes her hair, caressing her constantly. It seems that he resonated to Kate while we were at the fruit cave, and they are newly bonded. I cannot help but feel a small stab of envy for the one who is like a brother to me. He is younger than I am, and already has his mate and a family to come.

"Declawed? That's it? We're lucky they didn't do worse than that," Buh-brukh says in a practical voice. "I mean, they could have spayed all of us. They were trying to sell us as slaves and pets, so it stands to reason that we could have gotten out of things so much worse."

Kate just gives her a horrified look and clutches her small cat closer.

Taushen says nothing as the humans huddle together. Though he has grown increasingly silent and temperamental over the last few seasons, this is unlike him. Something bothers him, but he will not share it. He only watches Buh-brukh with a fierce expression. Perhaps he feels responsible for her. Out of all the captives, they were the only two kept in a cell together. Everyone else was separated.

Rukh is silent, too, though it is more because he is groggy. He is covered in bruises, and he was found unconscious. Suh-mer says that he probably attacked everyone when they separated him from Har-loh and his kit, and so they put him to sleep. Har-loh holds her son under one arm and clings to Rukh with her other arm, as if she can keep everyone safe by touching them.

Bek hovers over his Ell-ee, who is curled against his chest. Her eyes are big and frightened, but her panic has calmed now that her mate has returned to her side.

Out of all of them, I worry over Farli and Mardok the most. Farli's dvisti, Chahm-pee, was taken along with the others, to be sold like the snow-cat. He is freed and paws at the snow just outside the ship's entrance for food, unconcerned. But Farli has an arm around her mate's shoulders, and Mardok just seems...broken. There is a deep sadness in his eyes.

Suh-mer sits near him, offering her waterskin, but he shakes his head. "I'm all right. It's just hard. I can't believe Chatav and Niri, Trakan...all gone."

"Of course it is hard," Farli soothes, rubbing his shoulder. "They were your family, in a way. They would not want you to be sad. They would want you to be glad you live."

His smile is crooked, as if it is too hard to be happy. "They'd be pleased over one thing at least. Those bastards couldn't fly out because they shut me into one of the private quarters, thinking that because I was wearing furs, I was a native, too. So I just accessed my old override codes and locked 'em out."

"Then you saved everyone," Suh-mer says brightly. "That would make them happy—to know that you dicked over the guys that dicked them over."

"Small comfort," he says. "But I am glad that you and Warrek were able to rescue us. That couldn't have been easy."

All eyes are suddenly on us. Even small Rukhar is watching me. It is a curious sensation, considering I normally avoid attention. "It was all Suh-mer," I tell them truthfully. "She has a very clever mind."

Suh-mer gives a high-pitched giggle and waves a hand. "He's being modest. All I did was blab about chess and strategy for gameboards." Her voice is taking on the speedy inflection it does when she is nervous, and I wonder why. Is it because we have been linked together by the others? "I'd have been lost without Warrek's help. He did all the heavy lifting. All I did was sit around and brainstorm."

"You lifted the stone you put in the back of the ship," I tell her. "That was heavy."

Buh-brukh snickers. Suh-mer blinks at me.

"So what now?" Shail says. "Do we stay here? Send the ship into outer space?"

Suh-mer looks worried. "That might be hard to do. I sort of went a little wild with the laser gun and melted the control panels on the bridge so they couldn't take off." When Har-loh makes a dismayed sound, Suh-mer wrings her hands. "I didn't know things were already locked down! I'm sorry!"

I dislike that she is apologizing. No one would be safe if it were not for her quick thinking. "You acted to save the others, Suh-mer. You have shown nothing but bravery and strength for many days. No one should be upset over that. You have fought hard to rescue our tribesmates, and you even injured yourself without any thought to your own safety." I move to her side and glare at the others for making her worry.

"Well that explains where her eyebrows went," Buh-brukh murmurs.

"I wasn't criticizing," Har-loh says gently. "I would rather the entire ship be trashed than it fly off and us be separated from the others. I am beyond thankful that you rescued us." She hugs her small son close. "Believe me. It's just the tinkerer in me that hates the thought of losing so many working parts."

Mardok gets to his feet, brushing off his leathers. "We should double-check the ship anyhow. Make sure there are no stowaways from the pirate crew or any dangerous weaponry left around. We can also assess what the damage is and see how we can disguise that this ship is back here again. I don't want anyone else following it to our home and putting my mate—or the rest of the tribe—in danger."

I get to my feet, picking up my light-spear. "I am uninjured and well-rested. I will go."

"Me too," Suh-mer says quickly. "I want to help."

I shake my head. "You stay here with the others."

She frowns at me. "Why, because I'm a girl?"

"No, because you are exhausted and I want you here, safe."

Taushen gives me a curious look and gets to his feet. "I will join you and Mardok."

I nod. "That is enough. Everyone else stay here." I turn to Suh-mer once more. "Keep your light-spear at hand just in case."

That seems to make her feel better. She gets to her feet and shoulders it, a resolute expression on her face. "You got it."

She is far braver than I ever imagined, and I am full of pride for her. With my light-spear in hand, I head down into the hallway, followed by Mardok and Taushen. As a group, we head into each room and give them a thorough examination. Mardok seems to know all the secret places and tucked-away spots that an enemy could hide, and so we mostly guard him while he works. He is visibly shaken at the sight of the blood in the room he calls "med bay." In another room, he finds a colorful slate that lights up when he touches it. "The captain's data-pad," he says, voice sad. "Maybe he left behind a clue or two as to what happened." He touches the surface and then begins to tap at it with lightning-fast precision.

I wait by the doorway, giving him the time he needs. I can tell this is hard for Mardok, and I remember how I felt after my father Eklan's death. I wanted nothing more than to be left alone with my thoughts so I could grieve him without interruption and work through my shock and anguish. I want to give Mardok that same consideration.

Taushen moves next to me, leaning up against the wall. He has a spear tucked under his arm, though the ship is quiet and it will likely not be needed. He glances over at me after a long, silent moment. "You and Suh-mer hid in the fruit cave?"

I nod.

"I am curious about this," he says slowly. "Did she chatter your ear off with her endless words? She seems to talk faster and faster every time I see her. It must have made you frustrated."

"I like her voice," I tell him, unwilling to rise to his taunting.

"Mmm." He narrows his eyes. "Something is different between the two of you."

I grow tired of his games. "Do you wish me to speak plainly? I enjoyed her company, and being alone with her made me realize she is an attractive female and she has a clever mind. I have decided I am going to take her to my furs."

"A pleasure-mate? After all this time?" Taushen looks shocked. "But you've never pursued any females. Why now?"

"Because there is no sense in waiting for resonance if the right female has come along." Strangely enough, just thinking about Suh-mer and her flurry of nervous words, her smile, and the gleam in her eyes when she gets an idea—it makes me miss her. She is only down the hall, but I feel as if now that the others are freed from their imprisonment, we will not have a chance to be alone.

I will not let that happen, I decide.

Taushen looks struck by my words. "Not waiting for resonance," he murmurs, pondering.

"No," I say, and it feels more right the longer I think about it. I want Suh-mer in my furs. I want to explore her body and discover the joys of mating. I want to make her breathless. And I want it only with her and no other. "There is no need to wait. She would either resonate to you or me, or it will be many seasons from now. Why waste all that time when I feel strongly for her?"

"I did not think it was possible for you to feel strongly for anyone," Taushen tells me, a sly look on his face.

I ignore that. Does he think that because I am quiet that I do not feel as deeply as others? That I did not feel the pain of my father's loss, or that I cannot get hard when Suh-mer tosses her mane and the strands glide over her shoulders and touch her like I wish my fingers were touching her?

How does Taushen think I would not be attracted to her?

Unless...he wishes Suh-mer for himself. I feel a stab of jealousy and gaze at my friend with new eyes. Surely not. But Taushen also pursued Tee-fah-ni once upon a time. And he was close to Farli. And now there are only two females left, and he does not seem fond of Buh-brukh.

I have to fight the sudden urge to grab Suh-mer and haul her back to the fruit cave so we can be alone together once more.

But no. We must put the needs of the group first. It just means that I must remind Suh-mer that I have staked my claim upon her and show her my interest.

As long as she has not resonated, she can choose to go to my furs if she likes.

I will just ensure that she likes the thought very much. I feel a triumphant smile curving my lips at the thought. Suh-mer must speak her thoughts aloud to sort them. All I have to do is ask her how she wishes to be touched and she will tell me in great detail.

I look forward to that.

Across the room, Mardok makes a strangled noise.

"What?" Taushen asks, jumping to alertness. "What is it?"

I hold the light-spear tighter in my grip as Mardok continues to stare at the data-pad, shaking his head. "Something's wrong."

"What do you mean?" Taushen asks, impatient. "What's wrong?"

"The ship's logs. The last entries from Captain Chatav state that they dropped off their last shipment, and there are no other shipments recorded. The raiders wouldn't have used the captain's logs or updated them, but I know I saw cargo crates when they took us captive." He sets the pad down, a fierce frown on his face, and heads down the hall.

I follow after him, and Taushen is on my heels.

Mardok races through the winding halls of the ship and leads us to the large, echoing chamber that Suh-mer and I came in from. The ramp is still down, the bottom caked with snow. A breeze comes in from outside, cool and invigorating compared to the stale air on the ship. Mardok takes no notice of it, though. He is moving to the first of many of the oblong, dark shapes—"the crates," as he called them. "These shouldn't be here," he says, tapping his fingers on buttons. When it doesn't respond, he slams his fist against it and makes a noise of anger. "Kef! I don't have their password."

"I have this," I offer, and gesture at my light-spear.

Mardok looks up at me in surprise, and Taushen steps to the side, clear of us. "That might work," Mardok says. "It'll damage sensitive equipment, but I guess that doesn't matter at this point." He glances down the long row of crates, mentally counting them up. "There's at least a dozen here, and more in the next room. I'm almost afraid to open them and see what these guys were shipping."

"Shall I do it if you are afraid?" I ask.

Mardok gives me a rueful look. "Just a saying, my friend." He taps at the panel. "Shoot this, but not into the crate, if possible. Might be something useful—but really fragile—inside."

I nod and aim the light-spear like Suh-mer showed me. I tilt it so I am shooting straight down into the crate, instead of through it. The stone-like material melts underneath the light-beam, smoke curling into the air.

"That should be good," Mardok says, moving forward again. He has a bone knife in hand and wedges it into a seam in the crate, and then pushes down on it, levering the lid up. Taushen moves forward to help slide it off, and then the three of us stare at the contents.

It is a bubble. No, a pod. A watery fluid is encased in a see-through pod of some kind, and lights and blinking things—tek-naw-luh-shee, as Har-loh and Mardok call it—flick and catch the eye. There are wires everywhere.

But what catches my eye the most is what is inside the strange pod.

It is a female, with a dark mane and pale skin. Her eyes are closed, and she sleeps, strange cords hooked to her nose and another in her throat.

She is not sa-khui. She is not orange-skinned like the others. She is human.

"Kef me," Mardok breathes. "More slaves. That's why they were excited to find us. They're slavers." He stares in horror at the rows of dark crates, neatly lined up along the wall of the cargo hold. "Are all of these human slaves?"

Taushen and I exchange a look. A pit of dread forms in my stomach at what this means. Our life here, which has just settled down once more with the appearance of Ell-ee, Suh-mer and the others, will change again if there are many more human females. What will we do with them? Who will feed them if there are no hunters to mate to them?

What if...what if I resonate to one? Taushen's nostrils flare, and I know he is thinking the same as I am.

"We must speak to the chief," I say thickly. "Right away."

8

SUMMER

*M*ore human slaves.

It never occurred to me, in all the craziness that was going on, that the aliens would have even more slaves on the ship. And now all the aliens have been offed, the ship sabotaged by yours truly, and...we've got crates and crates full of people. Sleeping people, but people just the same.

I'm not the only one in shock. We've all gathered in the cargo hold, and everyone's silent as Mardok and Warrek pry off lid after lid to reveal the contents. At this point, I would have been thrilled to see a crate of weed or something, only because it would mean that it's one fewer person to get stranded here.

Harlow, Gail, and I talked with the other humans while the men were checking out the ship. We've agreed that we've got to do whatever we can to ensure no one comes after the *Tranquil Lady*. Harlow's going to work with Mardok to make sure we're not sending a signal of some kind, and she's going to insist that their first job is to disable the ship so it can never be used against us again. There are too many people at stake. We're in total agreement there. It's clear that if the ship leaves, someone's going to trace it back to this place, and if we leave here, we'll be separated. Even if some kindhearted (yeah right) alien decided to haul all of us back to Earth, I don't have any illusions that families would be kept together. Rukh, Vektal, and all the kind, strong sa-khui would be dumped in some Area 51-type place and experimented on to figure out what makes them tick. I can't even imagine what would happen to the kids.

This planet needs to be a one-way stopping point.

Of course, that was before we found more people.

"Another human female," Mardok says as he gazes inside the crate. We all pile in to stare at the person's face—not that we'll know her, because there are seven billion people on Earth, and half are female, but it feels weird not to.

"Okay," Harlow says, making a mark on the captain's data-pad that Mardok brought back with him. It's something like a tablet, and she's using it to record information. "That's sixteen human females and four alien males."

"That's the last crate," Kate says, petting the kitten in her arms as she exchanges a worried look with Harrec. "Should we wake them up now?"

"I don't think we should wake them up just yet," Mardok says.

"What?" Brooke gasps, shocked. "How can we not?"

"Each of these crates is set up to keep them in stasis for an indeterminate amount of time," Mardok tells her. He looks weary, and Farli is casting him worried looks. "For now, they're safe in here until we figure out what to do."

"We must talk with the chief," Taushen says, crossing his arms over his chest. "It is his decision. This is twenty more tribesmates that we must find khuis for. Twenty more we must feed and clothe before the brutal season, and already our tribe is larger than ever before."

"Yeah, well, we can't just leave them," Brooke snaps at Taushen. It's not the first time she's scowled at him today, and the both of them are making me tired just watching them.

I glance over at Warrek, but the look on his face is thoughtful as he gazes down at the sleeping human woman and then over at me. I try to imagine what he's thinking. Maybe he's imagining one of these women as a potential resonance mate. The thought makes me want to vomit.

And then another thought occurs to me. Some of the male slaves looked distinctly...intimidating. Fierce. Scary. "They might not even be friendly, Brooke," I point out. "We ran into these aliens and they attacked us. What if we free these people only to have them attack us out of fear—or something else? How do we know these alien dudes aren't cannibals?"

"Oh my god, Summer!" she exclaims. "What the hell are you thinking? They're people! They're trapped!"

"She isn't wrong," Gail says, speaking up for the first time in a while. "I'm with the others. We don't know these people, so we can't assume they'll be all happy and hunky-dory to wake up here."

"Safe," Elly whispers off to my side. I glance over, and she's clinging to Bek's arm, her expression worried.

The hard-faced hunter nods. "My mate is right. It is not safe for us, but think of them. How will we feed and clothe them on the long walk back to the village? It was a hard journey of many days for all the humans, and they are not prepared. We would need all the hunters to help bring so many over the land to safety."

"Then we do nothing without the chief's say," Farli says in a firm voice.

"But the chief is not here." Vaza strokes his chin, thinking. "Do we leave them all behind?"

"Some of us should stay to guard the ship and shut things down," Harlow says, putting a hand on Rukh's arm and then looking over at Mardok. "We have to make sure a second ship isn't going to trace this one."

Mardok nods. "We're on the same page. You and I have to stay, since we're the ones most familiar with the technology."

"I do not want to stay," Rukh says, speaking for the first time. His voice is flat, angry. "My mate is heavy with kit. I want her with healer." He pulls Rukhar against him. "Want my son back with tribe."

"We have to think about everyone, love," Harlow says softly. "I have to stay and work on the ship. No one is safe until we're sure that it's not transmitting anything." She pauses. "But maybe—"

"No," he growls. "You and I stay together."

She nods slowly. "But I do think Rukhar would be safest with the tribe." She looks heartbroken at the thought and hugs her son closer.

"If you want to send him back, I can take care of him," Gail offers. She approaches Rukhar and gets down on her knees, smiling at him. "Do you want to come on an adventure with Miss Gail?"

The little boy is silent. He looks at his father.

Rukh looks as if his worst nightmare is coming true. I'm surprised when he swallows hard and then nods, putting a hand on his son's head. "You go with Miss Shail. When we are together again, perhaps we find you a snow-cat like Kate's."

Rukhar manages a brave smile, but in that moment, I think he looks older and sadder than any of us. "All right, Father."

"Then that's settled at least," Harlow says, her eyes red and her smile tremulous. "We'll stay here to work on the ship, and Rukhar will go back with Gail and Vaza."

"And we're staying," Mardok adds, putting his arm around Farli's waist. She nods agreement with her mate.

"I'll stay, too," Brooke says, and I'm surprised. "Maybe I can help with whatever you guys need. If nothing else, I can try to assist. I don't know alien technology, but I was never terrible with computers."

Taushen scowls. "You should go back with the others."

"You should know you're not my keeper," she fires back and looks to Mardok and Harlow. "Is it a problem if I stay?"

"No," Mardok says, keeping his expression neutral. "It'll probably be useful. We'll need someone to run errands at least."

"It's settled then."

"We will go," Bek says, speaking up. He steps forward, but Elly doesn't stop clinging to his hand. "I want my mate back at the safety of the village. She is newly with kit, and I will not risk her further."

"Mine, too," Harrec adds. Kate makes a sound of protest, but the normally laughing Harrec shakes his head. "No. Kits are important. I will not risk you or my son."

I still can't believe they resonated. I still can't believe Kate got herself a mate while I was gone. It feels strange. Wasn't she just teasing me the other day about being boy-crazy? And now she's mated.

"It could be a daughter," Kate grumps, but she holds her kitten close to her chest and shrugs. "Well, if Rukhar's going back, at least I'll have someone to help me take care of Mr. Fluffypuff here."

The little boy smiles for the first time, and I feel my heart squeeze. Poor, serious little Rukhar.

"What about me?" Harrec protests. "I can help."

"Oh, baby," Kate says in a patient voice. "You'll be doing good not to trip over your own two feet."

A laugh ripples through our small group, and it somehow feels better. Less dire. I watch wistfully as Kate smiles at her mate and leans over to give him a kiss—she's tall enough that he doesn't have to stoop like the others do. I'm envious of how happy she is.

And of course, because I'm that dork, I glance over at Warrek, thinking about the conversation we had. I shouldn't be surprised that he's watching me, but I am. My cheeks heat with a blush, and I avert my gaze, but I can't stop smiling.

"What about you?" Brooke asks, and when I glance up, I realize she's talking to me. "Are you going or staying, Summer?"

I think for a moment. I'm honestly not sure. If I'm honest with myself, I want to go wherever Warrek goes. Of course, I'd never say something so obvious. I think about the groups that are staying and the groups that are going. It seems to me that the group that's leaving is the weaker one. Gail and Vaza will have Rukhar to watch over, and Kate and Elly will be accompanied by their mates, but they're also both newly pregnant. Not that I'm strong enough to tip the scales, but I've gained a new sort of confidence in myself in the last few days. Sure, I'm a blabbermouth, but I'm a blabbermouth with a *gun*.

"I'll go back to the village," I tell the group. "I might be more useful on the way back than waiting here."

"I will join you," Warrek adds.

Taushen just snorts, and I feel my cheeks getting hot all over again.

Harlow nods. "That's a good idea. We have enough staying here. In case any other ships land...it's best to have as many going back to the tribe as possible." She looks at her mate again.

Rukh shakes his head. "I stay at your side."

She leans against him, and he puts his arms around her. "I guess it's decided then," she says in a soft voice.

And it seems that it is.

"So when do we leave?" I ask, thinking about the journey ahead. It wasn't exactly fun to get here, because traveling through the snow is never exactly "fun," but the thought of slogging our way back for days makes me feel exhausted already.

"First thing in the morning," Bek says, brushing Elly's hair back from her face and caressing her cheek. She holds on to him tightly, and I realize just how terrifying this ordeal probably was for her. Out of all of us, Elly was a slave the longest. She's been happy with Bek, I think, but I can imagine the terror she's felt recently at the prospect of nearly being sold as a slave again. No doubt Bek's eager to get her away from here. Can't say I blame him.

"We have supplies back at the fruit cave." Warrek says in his quiet voice.

Harrec nods. "A small group of us can go and retrieve them while the rest of you stay here and prepare. I'm still strong. I can go."

"I'll go with you," Kate says.

Harrec shakes his head and tweaks his mate's blonde curls. "You stay here with the group. I will not risk you."

She looks frustrated, but nods.

"I'll go back to the fruit cave," I volunteer, though I'm exhausted, too. All of the adrenaline pumping through my veins for the last while has crashed and left me feeling like a noodle...but I also wasn't captured like the others. I'm healthy and strong enough— mentally and physically—to trek back across the valley and haul supplies.

"You will stay," Warrek says in a firm voice. "Rest with the other females."

I blush, but at the same time, it feels weirdly good to be included. And weirdly good to be singled out by him.

WARREK

It is late when we return from the fruit caves, our packs laden and the baskets piled high on a sled. It was surprisingly hard to leave the others back at the ship. I worried that with every moment we were gone, new enemies would appear and those waiting there would no longer be safe. Judging from how quiet Taushen and Harrec are as we work, I am not the only one that feels this way.

The return to the ship is equally quiet, as almost all the remaining tribesmates are piled into one of the larger chambers, beds close together. It is as if they all take comfort in each other. Farli and Mardok are at the center of the room, arms twined around each other. Kate is curled up next to Shail and Buh-brukh. Her small snow-cat is curled up on Rukhar's empty blankets, and Rukh's son is squeezed into the furs between his parents. Bek's mate is asleep off to one side, and Bek and Vaza both guard the group, weapons at hand, clearly unable to sleep.

Bek nods as we return, ever-silent. There will be more time to talk in the morning, before we set out.

I watch as Harrec steps over a few people to move to Kate's side. He slides into the furs next to his mate and puts his arms around her, holding her close, and she turns into his arms. I can hear the faint sound of their khuis singing to each other.

It fills me with envy. They are newly mated, and Harrec has always stated that resonance would forever pass him by. Now he has his Kate, and a kit on the way.

I think of Suh-mer. It has been very quiet without her endless chatter back in the fruit cave, and I found that I missed the sound of her voice, the steady stream of her thoughts. I search for her small form in the group and find her on the edge of the chamber, off by herself. As Taushen settles in with Bek and Vaza to guard, I wonder that I should not join them. I am unmated, after all.

But...why deprive myself? Why hold back from what I truly wish to do, which is to move to Suh-mer's furs and gather her in my arms?

Now that I have found her, why deny what I feel? I am tired of being solitary and alone. No one will care. Perhaps they will tease, but I do not mind that. Let them tease. I will have my female in my arms. Nothing else matters. I carefully make my way through the crowded chamber and move to her side.

She opens her eyes sleepily as I lie down next to her, gaze unfocused. "W-Warrek? Is everything okay? What—"

I put my finger to her lips, silencing her. "I wished to sleep next to you."

"Oh." She yawns. "Okay." She pulls the blankets over my hips and settles back down on the ground.

Greatly daring, I put my arms around her and draw her close to me. She fits under my chin perfectly, her form tucked against mine, and it feels better than anything I could have ever imagined. Her skin feels soft under my touch, and my cock stirs in response.

Now is not the time, though. There will be opportunities later. For now, I just want to hold her.

Suh-mer yawns again and leans against me, one hand curled against my chest. "'Night," she whispers, and I say nothing in response, waiting for her breathing to steady.

Eventually it does, and then I hear her soft mumbling. It is too low to make out what she says, so I lean in closer to hear her words.

"Just a little mustard," she murmurs. "No, I didn't say I wanted a sandwich. Just mustard. That's right. You can put it on the side of my plate."

Strange, though charming. I find it comforting that even in her sleep, she talks.

9

WARREK

The journey back from the Elders' Cave has none of the lightness of spirit that our original journey did. Harloh cries as she hugs Rukhar one last time, and her weeping puts everyone on edge. The sleds are packed, and Rukhar and Shail ride on the one Vaza pulls. Mine is loaded down with food and supplies, and my light-spear is now in Taushen's hands so he can guard the ship. Bek is at the front of our group this time, determination stamped on his face. He is ready to leave and get his mate away from this place.

The females are all bundled up with furs and snowshoes, Rukhar is hugged one last time, and then we leave. I remember on the first trip, Buh-brukh chatted with Suh-mer all the way here, but there is no lively chatter now. Kate walks alongside Harrec, her small snow-cat cradled in her arms, and Suh-mer walks to the side of my sled, quiet. She still carries her light-spear, though, and keeps it ready at her side.

I do not like how silent she is, though. It is not like her, and I want to hear her cheery voice. So I encourage her to speak, even if it means breaking my own silence. "Tired?" I ask.

Her cheeks flush a darker shade, and she shakes her head. "Just thinking about a lot of stuff. Am I quiet? Sorry. I guess that seems odd."

"What do you think about?" I ask, shifting the sled handles in my grip. It is not heavy, but I slow my steps so she does not have to walk as quickly to keep up.

"Just about those people in the pods," she says with a contemplative expression. "If they know they've been kidnapped, and if there's a reason why some people are being picked more than others. If they have families back home that miss them. If they're going to freak out when they wake up here and realize they're never going to see another summer. Things like that."

Never see another...ah. Her name means a warm season. I have only realized this just now.

"And then I wonder about the alien dudes," she continues, her snowshoes crunching in the snow. "Like, are they going to blend in with our tribe, or are they going to be all macho alpha male and try to mess things up? Are we going to have to split up? Because I kind of like the village and toilets. I can't imagine not having them. Well, I can, but I don't like my imagination to head in that direction. I try not to think about that sort of thing, if possible. And we've got the only healer, and what if they decide to split off from us and decide that they need the healer and..." She blows out a breath. "And stuff like that. Worst-case scenario crap. Basically, I'm running scenarios in my mind because I don't know what's going to happen. And...what if Brooke and I resonate to those aliens in those pods? What the heck do we do then?"

My hands clench on the handles, and I feel a surge of jealousy at the thought. "Did you feel a pull toward any of them?" I try to keep my voice mild, but it is difficult. Suh-mer is mine. I do not want her to resonate to another. Now, more than ever, I am glad she is traveling back with me. Let them all resonate to each other back at the ship and safely away from her.

"A pull? No. If anything, I kind of wanted to shut the lids and pretend we never found any of them." She gives me a rueful smile. "That's terrible, isn't it?"

"Not at all." I feel the same way. We had enough females for all unmated males. Why bring more and upset our tribe's balance? Then again, I suspect these people had no choice in the matter, just like Suh-mer and Buh-brukh and the others did not.

"But I'm just being a baby, I think. Everything has felt so unsteady ever since I was kidnapped that I was hoping the tribe would be the stability I needed. Now it turns out that everything's going to change again. And I'm sure they didn't choose to be kidnapped," she adds, echoing my thoughts. "And whatever life they have here is going to be far better than anything as a slave. I think I'm just panicking and hoping that if I think about it hard enough, some sort of perfect solution will show up."

I chuckle, because that does sound like her. "It is not our job to come up with a solution," I tell her. "That is the chief's worry. All we are tasked with is to tell him what has happened."

"Yeah, but it's got to suck being the chief with all these changes. If I were Vektal, I'd run screaming into the hills and never come back."

"He would not do that," I reassure her. "It is great responsibility, but he has a strong heart."

"Glad it's not me," Suh-mer agrees. "I'm happy being a tribe peon, thank you very much."

10

SUMMER

$\mathcal{I}$t's clear to me that after a full day of hiking in the snow, I'm not meant to be an outdoors kind of girl. It's kind of a moot point since I've been dropped on a primitive ice planet, but I'm pretty sure people like me were meant to live somewhere with a nice library, a cozy chair with a flannel blanket for my lap, and a space heater for my feet. Not snow, snow, endless snow and more snow. Not hiking across valleys and scaling rocky cliffs and plodding endlessly through the churned snow. After this, I think I'm not going traveling again. I like home far too much.

Funny that I thought the small stone huts back in Croatoan village were "roughing it." Ha. Ha ha. This is the universe teaching me that I never know how good I have things. I resolve that when we get back, I'm going to appreciate my cozy fire pit that I share with Kate and Brooke, and the toilet. Oh, the toilet, how I miss it so. You haven't experienced "roughing it" until you've tried to pee on the side of the trail while wearing snowshoes.

I like to think of myself as pretty decently in shape, but I'm no match for the day-long hike. It didn't seem this rough last time when we came this way...but then again, I remember riding in the sled with Brooke. I glance over at the others, and Gail's looking a little wilted, along with Elly. Kate's tramping along as strong as ever, and even Rukhar looks like he has more energy than me. I eye the sled Warrek's pulling, but I don't have the heart to ask to get on there. It's full enough already, and that'd just be a dick move.

I'm a little surprised when he slows his pace and moves back to my side. "Are you tired?"

I think about denying it and then decide there's no point. "I am. My feet are killing me."

He nods. "You look weary. There is a cave up ahead, and I suspect we will stop there tonight."

"Really?" I perk up at the thought. "How do you know?"

"Because Ell-ee looks tired, and Bek will not push her." His mouth curves into a hint of a smile.

I'm fascinated by that slow rounding of his mouth. Who knew that such a small movement could be so sexy? Not that I haven't been staring at his butt all day, or the long flutter of his hair in the wind. I never thought I was into guys with long hair.

Clearly, I'm wrong about such things, because damn.

He doesn't speak more, but he stays at my side, and there's a nice sort of companionship walking together, even if I'm too tired to burp up my normal endless stream of small talk. Sure enough, as we approach the nearest cliff, Bek signals to the others, Elly close at his side. "We make camp here tonight."

We all approach it, and my feet feel like they're getting heavier as I walk. I'm so glad to be done for the day.

The cave isn't exactly a paradise itself, though. I duck to get in and find that it's cramped, with barely enough room to fit all of us. It's dark, too, and the twin suns are going down.

"What about a fire?" Gail asks, teeth chattering. She puts her hands on Rukhar's shoulders, hugging the little boy.

"No fire," Bek says, a stubborn look on his hard face. "If another ship is coming, I do not want to signal to them where we are."

"Another ship? But it's been days," Gail protests.

"I will not risk my mate," Bek declares. "Vaza can warm you."

"I will be happy to," the older hunter says, his beaming grin just barely visible in the low light.

"And Rukhar?" she asks.

"I'm not cold," the boy says, moving to Kate's side to pet Mr. Fluffypuff.

"He is sa-khui," Bek tells her. "The cold does not affect him like humans."

"He's also half-human," she protests. "And what about Summer? She doesn't have a mate to keep her warm."

Oh jeez. I'm embarrassed to be singled out like that. Nothing makes you feel like a loser more than someone who's in a happy relationship pointing out that you're single.

"I will keep Suh-mer warm," Warrek declares. "Do not worry over her."

He will? A warm, shy glow sweeps through my insides. I thought maybe last night was just a fluke. That he was feeling the need to touch someone or have a little human contact, and I happened to be available.

I mean, he did make the big, ballsy promise that he was going to "claim" me once we made it out of this. We've officially made it to the other side, and here I am, sitting in the "unclaimed" corner still.

Not that I'm impatient or anything.

I'm determined to keep my yap shut through dinner. I think I'm too tired to talk. Well, mostly. I do chat with Rukhar about house cats and how we kept them as pets back on Earth. And I might have talked about the cats I had growing up, and how hoarders keep lots of cats because they can't bear to get rid of them, and that it might possibly be related to a parasite in cat urine that makes people want to own more cats and that I saw a news article about that once.

Okay, so I'm not too tired to talk, after all.

But I tell myself it's because Rukhar's such a solemn little figure. He's fascinated by the kitten, who's being fed a mushy mix of wet trail rations and jerky. Rukhar reaches for the kitten every time Kate sets him down. Kate's torn because she clearly loves the thing and wants to hold him, but who wants to take a kitten away from a child missing his mom and dad? No one. So Rukhar gets to hug and squeeze Mr. Fluffypuff as much as he wants.

We eat a cold dinner of trail rations and split one of the larger pieces of fruit between all of us. Then it's too dark to see, and everyone's too tired to chat more. Gail tucks Rukhar into bed, and he looks so sad and lonely that Kate immediately kneels at his side and hands him the kitten. That brings a smile to his sleepy face, and then we're all unrolling our blankets and getting ready for bed.

I'm so exhausted that it's hard to even unroll my furs, and when Warrek squats next to me and begins to undo the ties, I let him. I'm half-asleep when Vaza murmurs that he's going to take the first watch. Harrec volunteers to take the second, and Warrek offers to take the last.

Then I feel Warrek's large, warm body slide under the blankets with me, and I forget all about being tired.

He's down to nothing but his loincloth. When did that happen? I seem to remember him wearing leggings as we walked, because they had a decorative pattern down the legs and along the low-slung waist and I thought they set off the tightness of his butt rather nicely. Not that I was scoping his butt.

Okay, I was totally scoping his butt. But seriously, tails just draw so much attention to that area.

Now that I feel his bare, ultra-warm legs against mine, though? I'm wide awake. I remain completely still, just in case I'm being all weird over nothing. He might just be volunteering to keep me warm to be nice. He might be regretting the whole "I'm gonna claim you" business and is now hoping I don't bring it up. He might be—

He shifts in the blankets and slides closer to me, and then his nose rubs against mine.

"Suh-mer," he whispers, and his breath fans over my face. It's so unfair that I even like the way his breath smells. How is that possible?

"I'm awake," I manage in the barest of whispers. "What is it?"

"I wish to try kissing again."

"Right now?"

"Yes." He nods, and his horns practically bump against my brow. "Are you too tired?"

"Well, no! But there's a lot of people around—"

"They cannot see anything. It is very dark." His nose rubs against mine, and I swear, that starts a rather delicious tingle between my legs. "And we will be quiet."

Well, since he puts it that way... "All right."

"Tell me how to do it. Tell me the rules." His lips brush over my cheek, tantalizingly close.

The rules? I find it hard to focus when he's so close to kissing me. "There aren't any rules."

"Why not? Is there not a strategy?"

Is there a strategy to kissing? If there is, I don't know it. "You just do what feels good. Lips on lips, and then tongue against tongue."

"Ah, tongues. That makes sense. I have seen others do mouth-matings and wondered about it."

"Yep," I tell him softly, wondering if we're going to do mouth-matings or if we're just going to talk about it. For once, I'd rather not talk endlessly about things and do instead. His long hair tickles my arm, and I brush it aside, using that excuse to put my hand on his skin. Gosh, he's warm and delicious to touch. Maybe I'll just focus on what I can have instead of what I can't.

But then he shifts, ever so slightly, and his mouth brushes over mine. "I am surprised that there is no chess to this."

Chess? Does he mean strategy? I can't think, not with his lips carefully grazing mine. "It's instinct," I breathe. "All instinct. You just do what feels good."

His lips move against mine again, a cross between a nip and a kiss. "And does this feel good?"

Does it ever. I nod, and when I figure that's not enough of an answer, I give him a tiny kiss back. After all the mental lusting I've done over this guy—and planting a kiss of my own—it's like my courage has gone out the door and taken all my skill with it.

Not that Warrek notices, I think. His hand brushes against my cheek, and then he's angling my face toward his. And then our lips touch again, and this next kiss is deeper, and sweeter. Our lips linger, parted, and we just kiss, over and over again. Slow, soft kisses that seem like an appetizer for the upcoming main course. I forget all about how tired I am and everything that's happened in the last few days. I forget that we're squeezed into a cave with a bunch of other people and the only privacy we have is under the furs.

All I can think about is Warrek's mouth.

His wonderful, firm, warm mouth. And when each kiss grows deeper and I feel his tongue brush against mine, I open my mouth wider to accept it.

I'm startled when I feel the faint dance of ridges along his tongue. Ridges? But I shouldn't be surprised; his big alien body is covered in thicker, plated sections on his arms and thighs, back and chest. Of course he's going to have a few things different than me. I hesitate, but then he drags it against my tongue, and the results are so ticklish and arousing that I decide ridges are very, very good things.

For someone that has never kissed before, he's sure good at it. There's no awkward bumping of noses, no banging of teeth, no shoving his tongue down my throat. Everything he does is deliberate and with care, his fingertips lightly brushing against my skin as if he feels the need to touch me with every caress of his tongue. I'm utterly lost in sensation, and my world has shrunk to the firm, assertive flick of his tongue against mine.

I slide my arms around his neck, not only because it feels good to wrap myself around him, but because it allows me to press my breasts against his bare chest. I'm wearing my leather tunic, but since coming to this planet, I've gone braless, and my nipples are aching against the heavy clothing. I want to rub them all over him, graze them against his skin, and see how it feels when his tongue is dancing against mine in that seductive way.

He pulls his mouth from mine, and I give a soft little whimper of distress at that. "You are moving," he whispers, and flicks his tongue against my parted lips.

"Ignore it," I whisper back.

"Are you uncomfortable?" He smooths my hair away from my face and presses another kiss to my mouth, as if he can't quit me. I love that. I love everything about kissing him.

I shake my head. "Feels good," I tell him, keeping my voice as low as possible.

"Ah." His mouth claims mine again.

And then I feel him move his hand. First, it's at the hem of my tunic, and then I feel him slide it up under my clothing. His fingertips brush over my stomach, and then he's moving higher. His hand lands on my breast, and I feel him graze my nipple.

I can't stop the gasp that escapes me.

"If you are going to mate, mate quietly," Harrec calls out in a sleepy voice from across the cave. "Rukhar is trying to sleep."

Kate shushes him, and someone—Gail? Elly?—giggles.

I pull away from Warrek's mouth and bury my face against his neck in embarrassment. Oh my god. That's totally my fault—I was loud. I'm not sure I know how to be quiet. "Sorry," I whisper to Warrek.

"No apologies. I was impatient. We will wait for privacy." He gives me one more quick kiss and then presses his mouth to my forehead. "Sleep now."

"Yeah," Kate says, giggling. "Sleep now."

I'm totally going to smack her in the morning. If I remember, that is. Right now, all I can think about is how I'm supposed to sleep when Warrek's hand is still on my breast.

It takes everything I have not to squirm against that big, warm palm. Man, I can't wait for privacy, either.

11

SUMMER

*T*he next day, no one teases us at breakfast, at least. Thank god. Everyone eats quietly, packs up the furs, and then we're off walking again.

Today, the men walk near the front, the women in the middle, and those carrying sleds take up the rear. I'm pretty sure it's because we're slower than we were before, so the women are protected and can still set a slow pace. Harrec and Bek are at the front and keep an eye on how fast—or how slow—we walk and pace accordingly. Kate walks with me today, and she's got her kitten with her, tucked into a chest-sling so she can keep it warm under her tunic. Rukhar and Gail walk near us, and I can't help but notice that Rukhar watches Kate attentively. I'm guessing that if she gets tired of carrying Mr. Fluffypuff, he'll be quick to volunteer, even though Gail's holding his hand as we walk.

The kid's been pretty quiet this morning, and I feel bad for the little guy. He's only six years old, and this is his first time being away from mom and dad. Given all that's happened, he has to be scared.

So I try to draw him out with conversation. "Your mom and dad go back and forth between the tribe and the ship, right? Do you make this trip a lot with your parents, Rukhar?"

He nods, nearly as silent as Warrek. What is it with men on this planet and not being chatty? Goodness. Gail shoots me a troubled look and gives a little shake of her head.

Right, mom and dad are probably topics we should avoid. Luckily, Kate's front meows, drawing all of our attention.

She wriggles in her tunic, making a face. "I think Mr. Fluffypuff just peed on me."

Rukhar gives a little laugh, the first one I've heard from him. "Still want a kitten after hearing that, Rukhar?" I ask, teasing.

He thinks for a moment. "Yes, but I would like Mama and Father back more."

Oh jeez.

Gail shoots me a *shut up* look. Okay, so I'm failing with the kid. "Uh, so, um..."

"Rukhar," a voice calls out from behind us. Warrek. Our little group pauses, and Warrek strides closer to us, pulling his ever-present sled. "I need assistance. Will you scout for me? Look for rocks in the path and move them aside so I do not run over them?"

Rukhar brightens, smiling at Warrek. He races to Warrek's side and then begins to pick up the occasional small rock or stone that has been churned up by shifting snow, ice, or our snowshoes. There aren't many, and they certainly aren't big enough to stop someone as strong as Warrek. It seems an odd task until Warrek meets my gaze and he gives me another one of those slow, deliberate smiles, and I feel my body flushing all over.

Everything he does is with purpose, I remember. And he works with the kids back at home. Of course he'd know what would occupy a miserable child. It's not yakking about his parents with me. It's keeping him busy and making him feel useful.

"Catch up," Gail calls to me, and I realize I'm lagging behind our little group. I jog forward—well, as best as I can—and fall back into place between Kate and Elly.

"I'm glad Warrek's here," I tell the others.

"I'll bet," Kate says slyly.

I ignore that. Or try to. "I mean that he knew just what to say to Rukhar to keep him busy. He's good with kids. I think that's important, don't you? Not that I'm looking to have kids with him. Or that it's something even on the table. I just think for a guy, it's a good trait to have—patience and strength, along with a paternal instinct. Not that any of the other guys aren't paternal, but it's just different around him. I mean, maybe it's not but... Oh god, I'm babbling again, aren't I?"

"Mmmhmm," Gail says.

"It's okay," Kate says. "At least we know the truth about why your eyebrows are gone. They weren't burned off, they were licked off."

Elly giggles.

"Oh, you be quiet," I tell Kate, putting my mittened fingers to my brows. "My eyelashes are gone, too, and he didn't lick those. That would be weird. I burned them off all right. My whole face would have been one big blister except for the fact that Warrek had some really great cream—"

"Oh lord!" Gail exclaims with a shake of her head.

"Not like that. Face cream. Oh my god, you girls are *nasty*." When they all laugh, I bluster on. "It was a burn cream, you big ding-dongs. He rubbed it on my face—"

"That's what she said!" Kate howls.

I make a face as they all crack up. "Har de har har, yuck it up. You're not the one who looks like a big weirdo with no eyebrows."

Elly looks over at me and gives me a timid smile. "Still pretty."

Aww. Count on Elly to make two words feel like a gift. I beam at her. "And that is why you're now officially my favorite. These other chuckleheads can take a hike." I mock-scowl at Kate and Gail.

"I thought that's what we were doing." Kate pulls her tunic away from her chest and wrinkles her nose. "Okay, he didn't pee on me before, but he did now. I wonder if Harrec has a change of cloth-ing. Harrec! Babe!" She jogs ahead, clutching at the kitten inside her tunic.

There's a pause as we walk, and then Gail looks over at me. "All joking aside now, do we need to have a talk?"

"A talk? What about?" I give her a curious glance.

"Maybe not 'a' talk as much as 'the' talk. I think of you girls like my kids. I'm just trying to look out for you, and it's clear that after last night, you and Warrek got a little cozy back at the fruit cave."

I'm so mortified. "All we did was kiss, Gail! Jeez!"

"That's fine. I don't care if you do whatever you want. I just want to know if you're prepared for things. Are you a virgin?"

This is definitely the most embarrassing conversation I've had since being kidnapped by aliens. Possibly the most embarrassing conversation ever. "Yes," I tell her, words strangled. "Is it that obvious?"

"Maybe not to some. But I know what to look for. I was a mom, remember?" She smiles. "I'm not trying to make you uncomfortable, baby girl. It's just that we're on an alien planet and I'm wondering if we need to have a quick discussion about anatomy."

Oh, shoot me now. "I know how sex works, Gail. I don't think you can grow up with a TV or the internet and not know how it works."

"That's all well and good, but do you know *sa-khui* anatomy?"

Her emphasis reminds me of the surprising ridges I'd felt along Warrek's tongue last night, and I can feel my cheeks growing hot. "Is it very different?"

"Girl, have you never paid attention at the heated spring? They have an extra..." She puts her finger up and wiggles it. "You know." Her voice drops a little. "The spur."

I look at her, startled. How did I not know this? Boy, I really must not have been paying attention when people were bathing. "Spur?"

"It's a hard protrusion above the junk. Rubs you in all the right places, if you know what I mean." She nods at Elly, who has an equally mortified look on her face. "Elly here knows what I mean."

"Elly here's as embarrassed as me right now," I exclaim.

Poor Elly just chuckles, but she doesn't disagree.

"Okay, well, I'm just warning you so you don't scream your head off when you go exploring. Some of us like to sleep." She winks at me. "I won't give you the mom speech about getting pregnant, considering that he can't make you pregnant unless there's resonance."

Resonance—like what Harrec and Kate just went through. I picture my tall, robust friend and try to imagine her pregnant like Harlow. It feels like everything's happening so fast. "No resonance," I say softly, and I don't know if I'm happy or sad about that. I guess happy, but at the same time, I'd like to be the light of someone's life.

I'd really, really like to be the light of Warrek's life. Maybe that makes me a dork, but I don't care.

"All right then," Gail says, satisfied. "Just don't let your mouth make promises that your heart can't cash."

"I thought you were done 'mom-ing' me."

She gives me a sharp look. "Warrek is a good guy. He's sweet, kind, and devoted. All of these men are. Do you ever see anyone cheating on their woman? Not going to work? Standing around and drinking all day long and then demanding his woman make him a sandwich? These are good men. I just don't want you to play him, that's all."

"I wouldn't play him. I don't think I'd even know how," I protest.

"I know," Gail says. She pats my arm. "But I think you jump in without thinking from time to time, and that's why I wanted to say something. It's clear he likes you and you like him. But I think that these guys have a hard time with flirtation. To them, they go straight from holding hands and right to making a home together. There's no in-between with them. And it's a small tribe. You're gonna have to see his ass every day after this. Make sure that there's no bad blood between you."

Bad blood? "I wouldn't do that to him. I like him."

She sighs. "I know, honey. And I don't think you're the type. I just worry over my girls. Look at Brooke and Taushen. Something happened while we were kidnapped. They stuck those two in the same cell, did you know that? Everyone else got separated, but those two, they slapped together. Something must have happened, because ever since, they've been acting up at each other." Gail looks troubled. "I hope no one hurt her."

"Brooke?" I echo, surprised. Out of all of us "new" humans, Brooke has always seemed the most self-assured, the most comfortable in her own skin. The thought of her in distress is a painful one. I knew she was a bit snippy post-rescue, but I thought she was just tired and anxious—who wouldn't be after what they went through? "I hope it's just leftover stress from the trauma of being kidnapped."

"Me too," Gail says.

"Miss Gail! Miss Gail! Look what I found!" Rukhar races up to us and holds out a shiny bit of something. "What is it?"

She pauses and peers, exclaiming over it and making a big deal. "Well, that has to be the prettiest stone I've ever seen, Rukhar. That's amazing."

"Can I keep it?" He looks so excited.

"Of course you can." She smiles at him.

"I'm going to show it to Warrek," he says, racing off.

Gail watches him go with a soft expression, and I wonder how she's doing. She's so busy trying to take care of all of us that no one's stopped to see about her. "And you?" I ask. "How are you holding up?"

She shrugs. "I handle everything one day at a time. Today's a good day. Tomorrow, we'll see." She gives me a serene look.

"Don't you worry about me. I'm a survivor. If you want to worry about anyone, worry about that little boy. He's sweet, but my goodness, is he serious. I worry about that."

I watch as Rukhar pauses, then races up to Kate's side and shows her his new stone.

Gail chuckles. "I love that age. Everything's so exciting and the world's all new every time you turn around. It's so fun." Her laugh turns into a sigh. "It makes me miss my son. Sometimes I wish that Vaza and I could resonate. That I could be a parent again. I'm old, though. Isn't meant to be."

Elly's silent, and I cast around for something to say. Something that will help ease the old sadness in Gail's eyes. I don't know anything about children, or death, or what to say that will make it better. So I focus on something else. "Vaza? You want to have kids with him? Really?"

"Don't sound so shocked."

"I'm not. Sorry if it came out that way. I just thought you two were together for fun, you know? I didn't realize it was that serious."

"These men don't do anything but, remember?"

Elly gives a happy little sigh and nods agreement.

I think of Warrek and how he declared he was going to take me to his furs. Yeah, she's probably not wrong about that. "It is a pretty different culture."

"But a good one. Vaza's a good man. He treats me better than anyone's ever treated me before, and I was married for a long, long time." Her smile grows distant, fond. "Back when I was younger, I thought it was normal to have a marriage where you argued a lot, where you constantly felt stressed and worried, and as long as he didn't cheat on you or beat you, it was all good. But

Vaza's different. My husband was always the cleverest man in the room, and I grew to hate that after a while, you know? Especially when it's turned against you. It's nice to be with a guy that's a little more easygoing, who wants to do nothing more than spoil me as best he can."

Huh. I feel like I've learned more about Gail in the last three minutes than I have in the last three weeks. I think about what she's said and how these people seem to take to a serious relationship right away. I think about Warrek...and I think about resonance and how it might mess up what could be a really good thing between us. "What would happen if you resonated to someone else, though? What would happen between you and Vaza?"

"Ain't gonna happen, but it doesn't mean I'd boot Vaza." She shrugs her furs tighter around her shoulders. "When you love someone, you love them regardless of what a bug inside your body says. Sometimes I don't think they grasp that here, because it's easy to let the cootie decide. When you know, though, you know. Resonance would happen, but that doesn't mean we couldn't make something else work." She casts me a sly look. "Not saying I wouldn't be up for a little three-way."

"Oh my god! Gail!" I'm shocked. She seems so motherly.

Elly just chuckles.

"Pfft. Don't look at me like that, Summer." Gail wiggles her eyebrows. "Here's how I look at things. Losing my son and then being a slave made me realize that we've only got one life. I'm gonna live it to the fullest and enjoy myself and not gonna give a shit what others think. If that means I've got two men in my bed, if I'm happy and they're happy, who gives a rat's ass what anyone else thinks?"

Wise words.

12

WARREK

I am impatient for the day to be over.

Not because I weary of traveling. Not because the sled is heavy in my hands and grows heavier with every valley crossed. All of these things are true, but I have endured such things in the past and know that it is something easily borne. Not because I am ready to return to our chief and deliver the worrisome news to him—I am not looking forward to that part.

I am impatient for the day to end because I want to take to the furs with Suh-mer again.

The hunger to touch her is like a craving inside me, and it grows stronger with every day that passes. I find myself walking faster despite my heavy burden, just so I can hear the light, cheery tones of her laughter. I watch her figure as she walks, noting the sway of her hips with fascination. There is no tail to distract from the curve of her bottom or the way her body moves. Her mane flutters in the breeze, and I remember what it felt like against my skin, and my cock grows uncomfortably hard at the memory.

Mostly I think about last night and the soft noises she made when I kissed her. Even with my tongue slicking into her mouth, my lovely Suh-mer could not keep quiet. The hungry, breathless moans have haunted me all day. It makes it impossible to think of anything other than what will happen tonight. Will she welcome me back to her furs so I can touch the small buds cresting her teats? Will she let me kiss her more? Or will she be too shy around the others?

I do not want that to stop us from enjoying each other, I decide. If I must, I will pull her away from the others, if only to selfishly fulfill the need I have for her.

I crave the fragile, beautiful human. It is startling to me, but it also feels very right. I have been waiting for her, it seems. Now that she is here, and that she has shown interest in me, I do not want to wait any longer. Not for resonance, not for our journey to end, none of it. I want Suh-mer, and I do not care who knows of it.

Thinking of her and how I will touch her this upcoming night brings fierce pleasure, and I spend hours deciding how I shall touch her. Under her tunic, or shall I strip it off of her? Will I take the time to explore her with my hands, or shall I do so with my mouth? Can I use my tail to please her? What spots on her body will she like for me to touch other than just her teats? I wish to know everything.

I see now why my father was so broken over my mother's early death.

My father.

I have not thought of Eklan in at least a day or two. It is strange to realize that. I have grieved him, and grieved him deeply, since the day that he passed. I thought I would spend every day of the rest of my life aching for family, for all that I have lost. But with Suh-mer's bright, inquisitive presence, I no longer feel as alone as I did. I am sad for the loss of my father, but I no longer feel hollow that he is gone.

I wonder what he would have thought of Suh-mer, and I try to imagine what he would tell me if he met her. The thought is a... sobering one. *Never take a pleasure-mate,* I remember my father telling me once. *If you can spare yourself the pain of loss, do so. A pleasure-mate is a temporary thing—any female will go on to true-mate another hunter, and then you will be left alone. And that, my son, is the worst thing imaginable.*

My father would not approve, I realize with dismay. He would wish for me to avoid entangling myself with the lovely human, only so I would not be hurt when her khui chose another for her. He struggled far too long with the loss of my mother to ever see a mating as anything but the greatest pleasure—and the greatest of pain.

It is a pain he wanted me to avoid.

I should heed the wisdom of this but...I do not want to.

More than anything, I want to claim Suh-mer. I want her more than I wanted my first spear or a cave to call my own. I want her more than I want the next sunrise.

Even if it means I will live a miserable existence when she moves on from my furs, I will take that chance. Walking away without possessing her now is simply not an option. Not any longer.

～

WE TRAVEL SLOWER than expected that day, and by the end of the evening, there is no hunter cave in sight. It will be another night without a fire, though no one grumbles about it. A small blind canyon is chosen for our camp site that evening so we can sleep protected from the worst of the wind. Like the night before, everyone eats a quiet dinner of trail rations, splits a large piece of fruit, and then it is time to sleep. Rukhar curls up with Kate's little snow-cat, and the white-maned human does not seem to mind. She pulls a blanket around her shoulders, drags Harrec underneath it, and says no more.

I watch as Bek tucks his mate tenderly against him, a mountain of furs over her slender form. Vaza has buried Shail likewise, and only Suh-mer seems to be sleeping alone. She hesitates, then looks over at me, a question in her eyes.

But I have first watch this night. I move to her side, pull a thick fur wrap around her shoulders, and lean in to whisper. "I am on guard first this evening. Join me?"

She nods and gets to her feet, toting her light-spear with her as she follows me to the entrance of the canyon. We set up a short distance away from the others, and then I gesture she should sit on a nearby rock. She does, and I sit next to her, and we share blankets, watching the stars.

All is quiet between us, and even Suh-mer's normally endless chatter is gone. I want to touch her. My fingers—and my cock—ache with the need of it, but I dare not. Now, more than ever, the need for a watch is essential, and I will not put my need above the safety of others.

Despite my hunger for her, the evening passes pleasantly, and I am almost surprised when Harrec approaches and puts a hand on my shoulder. "My turn to watch," he says, yawning. "Go and sleep, you two."

Suh-mer gets to her feet, hugging the blanket around her shoulders, and looks expectantly up at me. I think for a moment and then put an arm around her and turn to Harrec. "We are going to take a few private moments."

He snorts and gestures a short distance away. "There's a smaller blind canyon in that direction. I'll keep an eye for you there, too. Just try to be quieter tonight than last night."

"You suck," Suh-mer tells him, but she slips her hand in mine. She wants to go, too.

We head to the spot Harrec told us about, and I set down the fur draped over my shoulders so she can have someplace to sit other than the snow.

Suh-mer shivers a little and watches me.

I worry this night is too chilly for her or she is too tired. "Do you wish to go back?" I ask.

"Not yet," she says softly, and moves forward and puts her hand on the center of my chest, over the hard plating that covers my heart. "I want to be with you."

I have been waiting all day to hear such sweet words. I drop to my knees and pull her down with me, until we are together on the fur and her legs are draped over mine. She is practically in my lap, her teats pressing against my chest.

Nothing has ever felt so very right.

Her arms go around my neck, and she wiggles a little. "Should I move? Am I uncomfortable?"

"You are perfect," I tell her, and my hands go to her waist. She is so small compared to the females of my tribe; the tunic she wears has been taken in at the sides, the seams thicker where the leather has been re-cut and reworked. I worry that I am too big to touch her without hurting her. Yet the others have taken human mates happily, some smaller than Suh-mer. Perhaps that is just my mind working against me. "May I touch you?"

She blows out a nervous breath, and it turns into a small laugh. "I thought that's what we were out here for."

"It is." I feel an urgent need to get this right, though, to make sure she wishes to return to my furs time and time again. Kissing her once was not enough. Twice only whetted my appetite for more. I want to touch her over and over again, explore every bit of her skin and see how I can make her gasp.

I must know more about her and her body. I touch her cheek, then smooth my hand down her shoulder, under the furs. "Tell me about humans."

"Uh, about humans?" Her brows furrow, and she tilts her head. "Well, we're about five feet tall, we have five fingers, and we're really bad at recycling. We like terrible movies and terrible fast food and equally terrible celebrities."

She speaks of nonsense things, and I can tell from the high pitch of her voice that she is nervous. My desire to make sure that I please her is making her uncertain. I must be clearer about what I mean, then. I put my hand on her thigh and rub, caressing up to her hip. "No, I wish to know what pleasures you."

"Oh." Her voice is very soft. Her gaze focuses on my mouth. "What, like clits and G-spots and stuff?"

"Those things, yes. All things. I want to know how to make you gasp when my hands are upon you. I want to know which touches make you shiver in a good way. I want to know how to make your body tremble until you break with the intensity of it."

"Wow," she breathes. "Those are a lot of words for a quiet guy. Might be the most you've ever spoken to me."

I continue to rub her rounded bottom, still fascinated after all this time by her lack of a tail. "It is because it is important. I wish to get it right."

"What we've done so far is pretty good," Suh-mer tells me, leaning closer. "I'm not an expert, of course. This is new for me, too. But I do like kissing, so we can do more of that, and maybe we can go from there. Unless you want a strategy to go about things, in which case—"

I cut her off, placing my mouth over hers in a firm, possessive kiss. Mouth-matings, most in my tribe call it, but to her, it is always a kiss. A she-spot and a clit, she also mentioned. I will remember these things. I want to know all that her body will crave, because I want to give it to her.

No female will ever be so well-pleasured as mine.

I pour everything I have into the kiss. I cup the back of her head, holding her close as I mate my tongue to hers. Previously, I was gentle, cautious with my kisses. This time, I hold nothing back. I drag my tongue along hers, slicking it against the smooth softness of her mouth. Even here, she is different—in so many pleasant ways—than I am.

Suh-mer makes that soft, needy noise in her throat, and my cock throbs in response. I feel a fierce surge of pleasure that I can make these sounds come from her, and I crave them as much as I crave the endless stream of her thoughts. Her scent is in my nose, her skin against mine, her slight form perched in my lap, and my senses are full of everything that she is.

No moment was greater than this.

Over and over, I slick my mouth to hers, consumed by urgency. Our time out here is limited, and even though I want nothing more than to leisurely explore her, I must bring her back to the others soon enough. Until then, I will take everything that I can.

She moans against me, and her weight shifts in my lap. Just that small movement causes her to rub up against my cock through the layers of my leathers, and it is as if I have been struck. I groan aloud, my hands tight in her feather-soft hair, and I press my forehead to hers, trying to compose myself.

"Warrek," she pants, her hands plucking at my shoulders. "Don't stop touching me. Please. I need more."

"I am not stopping," I vow to her. When her needy, sweet mouth moves over mine again, I drag my tongue over her lips and then ask, "Tell me I can remove your tunic and touch your skin."

She shivers, another breathless little moan escaping her. "Yes. Do it."

We break apart, and I grab the hem of her tunic. She raises her arms over her head, and I drag the leather over her head, then toss it aside as her beautiful form is revealed to me. Suh-mer shivers in the cool air, and I take one last, hungry look at the lines of her body before I pull her against me, warming her skin with my own. Soft. She is so soft everywhere. There is no protective plating on her body, no hard muscles on her form. She is all golden curves, her small teats thrusting upright from her chest. When she rubs her body up against mine, I want to lose myself in how good it feels to touch her and hold her against me. I slide my hands up and down her back, admiring how delicate she feels. "Too cold?"

Suh-mer shakes her head. "Your hands are warm. It feels good." She puts her arms around my neck again and boldly presses her front to mine.

"Tell me where to touch you." I cannot stop stroking her soft skin. "What places would give you the greatest pleasure?"

She squirms at my words, whimpering. "You're going to make me say it aloud?"

"Why would I not?" I lean in, unable to resist the curve of her jaw. I nip my teeth against it, and she trembles against me. "What is wrong with admitting what you like?"

"Nothing, I suppose. It's just very...bold for me."

"Are you not bold?" I tease along her jaw with small nips, stroking her back with my hands as I do so. "This is the female that took a light-spear and defeated several enemies. She risked burning her face and hands to stop the others. She rushed into the ship to protect me. Are these not the actions of a bold female?"

She moans and then drags her teats against my chest, her nipples scraping along my front. "Okay, you've got a point. Touch my breasts, then. Play with my nipples. And the undersides, because they're ticklish, too. Or, you know, just all of them. I'm not picky. Anything you do in that area will feel really good." Her words rush out. "But I really like it when my nipples are touched."

"I shall do all of that," I promise her. I slide my hands to her front, cupping her teats like she has requested. She is small here, unlike some of the other human females, but they are bouncy and rounded and jut forward, unlike the flat teats of the female sakhui. I decide that I like hers much better, especially the noises she makes when I touch them. I use my fingertips to lightly explore her, and it seems impossible, but her skin seems even softer here. I caress the rounded slopes of her teats, brushing over the undersides like she has requested, and she closes her eyes and sucks in her breath, her face tight. Her dark nipples are small and tightly budded, and I touch them, expecting them to be hard. They are taut, but just as soft as the rest of her, and this fascinates me. I stroke them lightly, and she makes a choked sound in response.

"Oh my god, you're killing me." Her nails dig into my shoulders, and she squirms in my lap, arching her back. "Warrek, please."

"Is this not what you want?" I whisper, a teasing note in my voice. I like her writhing and the tense look on her pretty face as I touch her. I stroke her nipples with my fingertips once more, and she practically shoves her teat into my hand with a whimper. "How can I make it better?"

She shifts in my lap, pressing higher. "Bite them."

Bite them? Take her teats into my mouth and nip at them like I did her jaw? It is a bold request, and one that nearly makes me spill in my loincloth. I groan low, holding her tight to me. "You wish for me to put my mouth on you?"

"Not hard," she says quickly, squirming against me. She arches again, and I realize she is trying to press her teats toward my mouth.

"Never hard," I agree. I would not injure her for anything. The thought of dragging my tongue over those soft, impudent little nipples has my mouth watering, though, and I lie back into the snow, pulling her over me until she straddles my chest. I put a hand to her lower back and guide her forward, but Suh-mer does not need encouragement. She thrusts her teats into my face, making little noises of pleasure.

How could any hunter resist such a temptation? I pull her down against me and put my mouth on her. At the brush of my mouth against her skin, her cries grow louder and she moves her torso back and forth, dragging the tip of her teat against my parted lips. I growl low in my throat at this tease, and anchor my hands against her, holding her still so I can nuzzle the delicious little bit of flesh. Her scent is incredible, the air perfumed with her arousal, obvious even through her leather leggings. I slide my tongue along her nipple, letting the ridges flick against her skin. She shivers and cries out, wild in my arms.

I love how fierce she is in her need, how she grabs a hold of my horns and pushes her teats against my mouth, demanding attention for them. She is the perfect female, my Suh-mer, and I am filled with a possessive lust for her. She is mine. No other male will ever touch her like this.

"Your mouth," she pants. "So unfair."

I growl low, because I want to drag her hips down to my cock and press the hard heat of my arousal against her cunt. She wants unfair? I want to be deep inside her...but the need to pleasure her overrides everything. "Shall I stop?" I ask between licks, nipping at her teats and careful not to use my fangs.

"Noooo." Suh-mer moans and then slides down my chest. She claims my mouth in a fierce, tongue-tangling kiss. "I just...need a moment."

I return the kiss, licking and teasing at her full mouth like I did her teats. She shivers when I nip at her lower lip, and I decide she's had long enough to rest. "Tell me how I should touch your..." I think of the things she told me. "Clit."

Her moan is low and desperate, and she closes her eyes. It is almost as if the thought is too much to bear.

"Where is it?" I ask between kisses. "Show me, and I shall caress it."

Suh-mer's mouth is desperate on mine, as if she wants to tell me but cannot bring herself to do it. I do not understand this shyness, but now I want to touch her in her favorite spots more than ever. "Is it near your cunt?" I ask, guessing. Humans can be shy about such things.

Her little moan tells me that I have guessed correctly. I remember Vektal and a few of the other mated hunters mentioning a third nipple. "Between your folds," I murmur, and she nods, burying her face against my neck. "Will you like it if I touch you there?"

"Yes," she chokes out.

"Then I shall do it." I hold her against me and roll our bodies on the furs until she is under me. Her leather leggings are drawn up and knotted at the waist, and when I tug at the string, they fall open, loose on her slight form. Her belly quivers as I skim my fingers over her navel, and then I pull her pants down lower, exposing the tuft between her thighs. The scent of her arousal envelops my senses, and my mouth waters. I hunger to touch her more, to taste her. They say there is no sweeter flavor than a reso-nance mate on a hunter's tongue, but I suspect that Suh-mer will taste just as sweet. I do not think I could want a female more than I want her in this moment, and I slide my hand down to my cock, pressing against it to force my arousal down. Right now, what is important is her and learning to pleasure her. My pleasure can be ignored until later, and if she is not ready to mate, I will take myself in hand and relieve the need. I will not rush her.

Everything will be as she wants it.

Suh-mer gazes at me with hungry eyes, sucking in her breath as I let my fingers trail down her stomach. I will not rush this, since the anticipation is part of the sweetness of the moment. I love the noises she makes as she waits for my touch, breathless and keening and impatient all at once. Even though she is not speaking her thoughts aloud, I can guess them by the sounds she makes, and they guide me as much as any spoken word. She trembles as I move my hand lower, and I stroke her curls lightly. "Show me where your clit is, or shall I find it?"

She makes a noise in her throat and closes her eyes, then slides her thighs apart in a way that is both shy and bold all at once. I watch, fascinated, as she spreads her legs, revealing her wet cunt to me. She is a darker gold here, all flushed skin and slick folds, and I want to touch her—to bury my face there—more than anything. I clench a fist at my side to steady myself, determined only to watch as she moves her hand to her cunt and parts her folds, then slides one finger in a slow, deliberate circle around a tiny nub of flesh.

The third nipple. Her clit. It is barely visible, tucked neatly into the seam of her cunt, but now that I know my goal, I am eager to pleasure her.

It takes everything I have not to push her hand aside so I can greedily put my mouth there. I am salivating, watching as she touches herself. "My brave Suh-mer," I murmur, because I can tell she is shy. "You are lovely."

She moans in response, shuddering, and pulls her hand away. It gleams with wetness from her thighs, and I cannot resist. I capture her hand in mine and bring her fingers to my mouth, tasting her.

It is like nothing I have ever experienced before, and I am lost. I groan, cock surging in my leathers as I lap up her musky flavor. "Your taste, Suh-mer. There are no words."

"I can't believe you just did that," she whispers, squirming.

"Can you not?" I press a kiss to each delicate fingertip. "All it has done is made me crave you even more." I glance down and see she has drawn her legs together reflexively. I bend over her and put my hand on her knee, pressing a kiss to the inside of it. "Will you be nervous if I taste you again?"

"You want to?" She gives a tremulous little sigh and moves to put her hand between her thighs again.

I stop her and press my mouth to her knee again. "I would taste from the source."

Suh-mer moans again and presses her hand to her brow, as if the thought is too much for her to handle.

"You can tell me to cease at any time," I promise her, and kiss down her thigh, slowly tugging her legs apart as I do. Here, her scent is mouthwateringly strong, and it takes all of my willpower to kiss gently down her leg instead of flinging her thighs apart and ravishing her with my mouth like I want to.

I am the most patient of males, I decide as I kiss lower. The most patient, or the most foolish for not moving straight to her third nipple—her clit.

But then my mouth is hovering a breath away from her folds, and her noises are growing louder, needier. I can wait no longer. I touch her with one careful thumb, dragging it down the seam of her cunt from top to bottom, watching her reaction. She jerks in response, her back arching, and her thighs go wider.

She wants more.

That is what I want, too. With my thumb, I part her folds and reveal her gleaming, flushed cunt to my hungry gaze. I lower my head and give her a long, savoring lick.

They are right; it is the best thing I have ever tasted, and far sweeter being licked from her skin than her fingers. I groan, rocking my cock against the furs. I cannot help myself; the need for her is too great. Nor can I go slow any longer. I press my mouth to her flesh and taste her with all the urgency building inside of me. I lick her with sure, slow strokes of my tongue, careful to lap up every bit of moisture. I suck on her clit to make her cry out, and then trace my fingers over her, exploring her and finding ways to wring more pleasure from her.

But she has not shuddered with release yet. I must give her more. "Where is your she-spot?" I ask between hard, deliberate licks.

She cries out, no longer quiet or even trying to be, rocking her hips against my face. "M-my what?"

"Your she-spot," I tell her again, flicking my tongue against her clit in a way that makes her entire body jump. "Tell me where it is and I will pleasure it, too."

"Oh god," she moans, flexing her hips again. "Warrek, no, it's okay—"

"Tell me or I will stop," I demand, then circle the tip of my tongue around her clit.

She gives a low cry. "God, you're such a dick." When I raise my mouth from her cunt, her hands go to her teats and she frantically rubs at her nipples, trying to come. I capture her hands in my larger one, and she writhes under me, frustrated. "Warrek, please!"

"She-spot," I demand. I *need* this. I need to watch her achieve her release.

Suh-mer closes her eyes, panting, and seems to be trying to calm herself. I do not want that. I want her to come. I push my face between her thighs once more and lick her long and hard, until she's wriggling underneath me once more, her hands fighting to get free from mine.

"Okay! Fine! You dick. It's a G-spot!"

"That is what I said. A she-spot." I press a kiss to her mound. "Tell me where it is so I can lick it."

Her moan is throaty. "You—you can't lick it. It's inside me."

Inside? Humans are fascinating. "Where? How do I get to it?" I lift my head and examine her cunt. I have not pushed into her core yet, nor her bottom. "Tell me, or I shall start finding it for myself."

Suh-mer takes a deep, shuddering breath. "It's...so, I don't know for sure, because I've never found it on myself, but it's supposed to be a small, rough patch of flesh on the inside of my, well, my hoo-ha."

"Your cunt?"

"Sure, if you want to get all crude about it." She sounds distracted. "On the inside wall, just below where my clit is, I think. It's like that nerve area is connected or something. I don't know if it works for everyone, but I've heard it's supposed to be incredible and—"

Her words cut off with a gasp as I push a finger inside her core. She is slippery and hot here, her cunt sucking tightly at my large finger, and I imagine this sensation around my cock and grind my hips into the furs once more. Such pleasure...no wonder hunters lose their heads over their mates.

"Warrek," she breathes, her eyes heavy-lidded with pleasure.

"Stay still," I tell her, concentrating. If this is the secret to making her wild, I want to discover it. Not that she has not already been pleasingly aroused—the slickness between her thighs and her needy keening tell me that she is—but I want to do more. I slide my finger deeper into her warmth, stroking her like I want to with my cock.

"Oh, Warrek." She raises her hips, meeting the thrust of my finger. "God, that feels so good." Her eyes close and her head tilts back, a look of bliss on her face.

"Is this your she-spot?" My breathing is raspy now, too, my control on the very edge.

"I—I don't think so? It feels good, though."

Hmm. I drag my finger up and down, thrusting gently. I do not feel a rough patch. She is all smooth wetness inside. I gaze down, considering. The underside of her clit would not be as deep as my finger is inside her. Perhaps I need to start over. I pull out of her, and she makes a low whimper of protest. "Shhh," I murmur, leaning in to give her clit another lick to satisfy her. I cannot resist another taste. I put my finger to the entrance of her core and gently push in, just a little. The walls of her are harder to touch at the entrance, though, and so I crook my finger, looking to drag the pad of it along the inside of her cunt. Still smooth. I go a little deeper—

And feel just a tiny hint of texture.

Suh-mer makes a choking sound. Her hands fist in my mane, and she wheezes, her entire body trembling.

I think I have found out. I glide my finger over the spot again, and use my tongue on her clit. She arches again, a cry breaking from her throat. When I rub the she-spot again, her cry gets louder, until it echoes off the cliffs around us. Her hands are tight on my mane, and she thrashes her head back and forth, body trembling. "Warrek! Oh—my god! Right freaking *there!*"

I rock my hips against the blankets, her need making my own hard and furious. I want to bury myself inside her, and I can feel the feral growl of hunger rising in my throat. I thrust against the blankets, using the friction of the snow and the furs to give me what little pleasure I can take.

"Wait, wait, wait," she says breathlessly, but her hands grind my face against her cunt as I continue to rub her she-spot. "Warrek! Oh! Oh! Oh!" Her voice becomes louder with each cry, and it feels as if she is tugging fistfuls of my mane out, but I do not care. It only adds to the frantic edge of our pleasure. I flick my tongue against her clit with renewed enthusiasm, wanting her to collapse with satisfaction.

"Ho, Warrek. Is everything well—"

A voice. Someone intrudes.

I lift my head and snarl, half-feral, as Harrec approaches. He dares to near my mate? "Leave us," I growl.

The hunter's eyes go wide at the sight of us—Suh-mer splayed on the ground before me, and me with my mouth—and fingers— between her thighs. "Apologies. I was just making sure, because it got very loud—"

"Leave!"

"Going!" Harrec chuckles and dashes away with a strange little hop.

"Warrek," Suh-mer demands, a needy note in her voice. "Please—"

I lower my head and give my female—no, my *mate*—what she needs. After this, I am never giving her up. Suh-mer is mine. And in the next few moments, when she screams my name with fierce satisfaction and her cunt clenches around my fingers, I feel a sense of pride and possessive hunger I've never felt before.

My mate. Mine.

I press a kiss to her sweet, black-tufted mound. It is wet with her release, and her body trembles against mine. "Cold?"

She moans. "God. Warrek, I...you..."

"Yes," I agree. Her. Me. Together. Always.

It is as it should be.

SUMMER

So my first time with a guy and I totally squirted. I'm pretty sure he finger-banged the brains out of me. It feels totally crude and a little bit naughty to think about that, but I can't help it. I'm still dazed and thinking about being with him the next day when we wake up and make ready to break camp. I've kind of kept to myself for the most part, but whenever I look at Warrek, he has a secretive, almost self-satisfied smile on his face that broadens every time I blush.

Yeah, someone's feeling good about himself this morning. He's not the only one. I haven't felt so...happy in days. Weeks? Months?

Ever?

I don't even mind when Bek sighs at the gloomy skies. "Going to be a long, snowy day."

That's all right with me. Bring it on. And when Warrek moves to my side and drapes his shoulder-wrap over my body, it feels like a declaration of ownership.

And it makes me think about his face between my thighs and how everything pretty much just went from a seven all the way to a twenty-something on the Richter scale. Does the Richter scale even go that high? Maybe they need a hoo-ha scale.

13

WARREK

*H*arrec jogs back to my sled at about midday, a huge grin on his face.

I say nothing, keeping my expression carefully blank. I can guess what he is about to ask about. Perhaps I should apologize for startling him, but no. I will not apologize for making my mate scream with pleasure. For making her cunt grow wet with her release. I will never apologize for these things...because I intend on making them happen on a regular basis.

"Can I walk with you, my friend?" Harrec moves to my side, not waiting for an answer.

I nod. Today, my sled does not feel so heavy, nor the walk so long. The weather is dreary, but it cannot bring down my mood. I am... happy. And as I watch Suh-mer walking ahead, chatting with the other human females, I realize that she is the reason for my mood.

She makes me happy. It is a good feeling, and one that almost feels shameful after the recent events. Bek's Ell-ee still wakes up with nightmares, and I know Har-loh and Rukh are upset at being separated from their kit. I know Mardok grieves the loss of his old tribe, and Farli worries over him.

But I am happy.

I am not the only one, either. Harrec keeps grinning at me, a curious look in his eyes.

"What?" I finally ask when he does not speak up.

"I interrupted some very interesting play last night," he says casually.

"You did. I told you where we were going."

"Yes, but you did not tell me she would make noises as if she were dying." He smirks at me. "It is a good thing you did not return to the fire to play fur-games with her."

I snort, but I also cannot stop the smile that curves my mouth. My mate was indeed rather noisy. It means I did my job well. "Tonight, you will know not to come looking."

"I will not," he agrees. "But I am curious what you were doing to her. My mate is noisy, I thought, but not quite like that."

I ponder for a moment if this is a secret, then decide that likely, it is not. I am one of the last males to experience a romp in the furs with a female. Surely they have all made their mates come, and come hard. "She likes her she-spot to be touched."

"Her what?" Harrec pauses.

I do not. I continue pulling my sled, glancing up ahead at Suh-mer. She's exclaiming over something that Rukhar shows her, tucking her soft, soft mane behind one small ear. Such pretty ears, too. I wonder if she would like for them to be licked—

"Her what?" Harrec demands again, jogging back to my side.

I glance over at him. "Her she-spot."

His expression is no longer laughing. "You mean her third nipple?"

"No. That is different."

He elbows me when I do not provide more information than that. "What is it, then? I wish to know."

"Do you not already know of such a thing? It is a place that she likes to be touched."

He shakes his head, eyes wide. "Tell me more. I wish to make my Kate scream like a snow-cat in heat."

"I do not know if I should say. Perhaps it is something Suh-mer does not wish for me to speak of."

Harrec exclaims loudly, causing all the females to turn around and stare at us. They pause, and Suh-mer blushes at me before turning around, and I smile once more.

"You cannot tell me of a she-spot and then not share this! I want to pleasure my mate like that, too. Where is it at?" He sucks in a breath and then puts an arm around my shoulders, causing my sled to tilt wildly. "Did you put something in her bottom? Is that why she screamed? She was outraged?"

I shove him away, annoyed. "Even if I did, I would not tell you. And did she look outraged to you?"

Harrec frowns, studying my brow.

"What?" I ask, righting my sled and continuing forward.

"Did she pull out a tuft of your mane?"

Did she? I pause, setting down my sled and touching my brow. It is tender in one spot, the threads ragged. I chuckle at the realization. "Perhaps she did."

Harrec moves in front of me and puts both his hands on my shoulders. "You must tell me this secret. I need to know about this she-spot. Right away."

I think for a moment, and Suh-mer glances back at me again, a little smile on her mouth. She is so beautiful it makes my heart ache. Touching her was such a great pleasure, how can I not wish for Harrec to experience the same with his Kate? "It is a rough spot," I begin.

"Tell me more," Harrec says, an intense look on his face. "I wish to learn."

SUMMER

It's a few more days of arduous walking before we make it back to the tribe. I don't remember the journey there being such a pain in the butt, but the hunters are pleased with the time we've made, so maybe it's just me. All I can say is that I'm beyond relieved when I see the plumes of smoke on the horizon that signal the cookfires of the village.

But I'm also a little worried about what happens with Warrek now that we're home.

I mean, it's pretty obvious to everyone at this point that we're a couple. We walk together a lot. We curl up with each other under the furs to share warmth. He offers me his waterskin and brings me his portion of the shared fruit (he's not a fan of the sweetness). And every night, we sneak away together for a little bit to get some "alone" time.

I love being with him. I can't imagine spending this time with someone else. And sometimes I feel guilty that I'm enjoying his company so much when there's so much dire crap going on. We've got alien ships landing when they shouldn't, I shot my fair share of slavers, and now we've got twenty new slaves to think about possibly integrating to the group.

I shouldn't be happy. But...I am.

I like Warrek a lot. I like his smile, his frown, I like his long, long hair. I like his horns and his blue skin. I really, really like his butt and abs. But mostly, I like his thoughtful personality. I like that he's quiet and deliberate in everything he does. I like that he listens to everything I have to say—and boy, do I always have a lot to say. I like that he doesn't try to shut me up or interrupt me. He acts like what I'm saying is the most important thing ever, and when he comments or adds to my thoughts, I know he's paying attention. We've talked about everything from hunting strategies to chess, and he's going to make a board when we get back to the village so we can play together.

I guess we're back now, though, and the thought makes my stomach quiver with nerves.

I should be worried about how Vektal and Georgie—our leaders —are going to feel about the new humans and the fact that slavers showed up again. Instead, all I can think about is last night, when Warrek kissed me long and hard as he slid a finger in and out of me, finding my G-spot again.

I came at least three times. In a row.

I should have done the same for him. I'm dying to touch and explore him, but every time I suggest it or reach for him, he distracts me. Says we don't have enough time for both of us to get pleasure and he wants me to have it. But it's starting to make me feel downright greedy. He loves pleasuring me, but I really want to give back to him. We just need the right place and enough time for me to tackle him.

And now that we're heading back toward the village, I wonder if we'll get it. I worry that things will be so crazy that we're going to get lost in the shuffle and this thing we've got between us—this fragile bond—will snap like a twig.

I hate the thought. I need more than just a few kisses and furtive gropings. I need...him. His steady, calm presence that soothes my jitters and makes me feel like everything's going to be all right, no matter what.

But then we're heading down the pulley and lift, pausing so the sleds can be lowered and nothing left behind. Scavengers—and the rare roving metlak—will make short work of our supplies, so they have to be protected. That's fine with me. I've got no one waiting to greet me back at our small hut. The only person I want to see is pulling a sled, so...

Everyone's distracted today, though. Maybe it's that we're about to end our journey, or maybe it's that no one really wants to break the news that we've got a new problem, and a big one. Whatever it is, I half-expected a few people to gallop to the village, but everyone seems to be clustering together, as if we don't want to separate. Even high-spirited Harrec is hovering around Kate, fussing over her as if she's as delicate as the rest of us.

The sleds are at the bottom, then, and there's no reason to stall any longer. We fall into our regular walking patterns, and Vaza picks up Rukhar, who's tired of walking after so many days, and rests him on his hip. "Almost there," Gail tells him. "Then everyone can take a long, long nap."

A nap. I'm tired, but I'm not thinking about sleep. I'm thinking about Warrek. Tonight, he's not sleeping next to me. He sleeps with the other unmated hunters in one hut at the edge of the village, I think. I never paid much attention before. I share a hut with Kate and Brooke...except Kate is now mated to Harrec, and Brooke isn't here.

Gonna be a lonely, cold night for me. Maybe I should ask Warrek if he wants to sleep over. Maybe—

"Ho!" a booming voice calls. In the distance, deeper into the ice canyon, a big blue guy raises a hand in the air. A stout blonde human waves, and I realize it must be Hassen and Maddie.

"Ho!" Bek gestures back, and then they jog forward to meet us.

"Look at all of you," Hassen calls, laughing as he approaches. "Tired and bedraggled to a one!" His face sobers as he sees Vaza carrying Rukhar, and glances behind us. "But...where are the others?"

"Everyone is alive and well," Bek tells him. "Do not panic. But we must speak with Vektal immediately. Where is our chief?"

"He is with Shorshie and the elders. What is it?" He moves to Warrek's side and grabs the handles of the sled from him. "Let me, my friend. You have had a long journey."

"Is everyone okay?" Maddie asks, her worried glance bouncing from face to face. Her gaze rests on me, and her eyes widen. "What happened to your eyebrows?"

Damn it. I was hoping they'd grown in a bit. I touch my face self-consciously. "It's part of the long story." More threatens to spill out of me, but Warrek puts a calming hand on the back of my neck, and I bite it back. I sure don't want to be the one to break the news to everyone.

Maddie and Hassen shoot us worried looks, but they manage to hold their questions until we get back to the tribe.

Even though everyone in the tribe has their own little stone hut and there are several cookfires in the main "road" of the village, people tend to gather in the big longhouse at the far end of the village. It's got the pool that's fed by a hot spring, room to stretch out and do crafts, and everyone hangs out there. Vektal tends to hold his "meetings" there when he talks with others. I know he and Georgie like to make the elders feel included, and so they often have discussions with them there. When we don't stop at any of the houses, I know our little group is heading right for the longhouse. I feel a sense of unease with every step. People are popping their heads out of their houses and stopping to look at us, but no one approaches. It's like everyone knows there's something up. Maybe our faces are giving that away.

No one splits off from our small group, either. It'd feel traitorous to abandon the others, I think. Instead, we all head toward the longhouse to deliver the strange news.

I'm at the front of the group, and when I enter the longhouse with Gail, Vaza, and Rukhar, I see Georgie and Vektal get up from their seats where they're meeting with Drayan, Drenol, and Vadren. Their warm smiles fade as we file in, and my stomach knots up.

"I'd ask how the trip was, but...why's Rukhar with you? Where are Rukh and Harlow?" Georgie asks, clutching at Vektal's arm. "You guys are scaring me."

"There is much to tell," Bek says, glancing at the others and then stepping forward. "But all are alive."

Georgie's eyes bug at that, and her grip on her mate's arm gets tighter.

"Perhaps do not start the story there," Warrek says in his calm voice.

"Then where should I start?" Bek snaps. "Where the alien ship landed and tried to enslave us all? Or where you and Suh-mer attacked them with light-spears and almost got killed? Or the part where Mardok's old tribe is dead?"

"What?" Vektal demands. He stares at each of us, a fierce scowl on his face. "What are you all speaking of? What has happened?"

The pressure becomes too much for me. "We found new humans," I blurt out.

Georgie gasps. "New humans?" Her face goes pale. "How?"

Someone shoots me an irritated look, but I can't stop the waterfall of words coming out of my mouth. "So the ship was taken over by bad guys, and then they tried to steal the others, but I guess that's not what you're asking, right? Anyhow we went to save them, and we found a ton of crates, and we were like, gee, that's odd that there are crates, and so we had Mardok open the first one up and it turned out there was a person, and the guys that offed the old crew of the *Tranquil Lady* were slavers, and when we beat them—well, 'beat' isn't the right word I guess, so killed might be closer, but whatever—and we took their shit, I guess we got their slaves, too." I suck in a deep breath. "And to make a long story short, there are, like, sixteen humans and four aliens. And we don't know what to do with them, so we thought we'd come to you guys."

You could hear a pin drop.

Gail politely clears her throat. "What she said, I guess."

"Twenty humans?" Vektal echoes. "Did I hear you right?"

"Sixteen," Warrek corrects, and he squeezes my shoulder. I guess that's code for "shut it, Summer." Can't blame him. I'm feeling a little embarrassed that I just burped up all that. Seriously, though, someone had to say something. "And four that look like fierce hunters from very different peoples. Males."

Georgie faints.

Vektal roars, catching his sagging mate before she falls to the ground.

After that, not much is getting done, sad to say.

I really need to work on my subtlety.

14

SUMMER

We're all a little panicky until Vektal emerges from his hut and returns to the longhouse. "My Georgie is resting," he says. "Maylak will stay with her."

"Is she all right?" Gail asks, seated on the floor near the fire. Kate, Elly and I are seated next to her as well, and the men have formed ranks behind us. It's like they're trying to protect us, which is sweet, but I'm not sure what we'd need protection from at this point. The elders have cleared out, though Harrec joked that they just wanted to be the first to gossip about what's been happening. Rukhar sits in Gail's lap, which is kind of funny because as a sa-khui kid, he's a lot bigger than most his age, but she tucks him under her chin like his legs aren't almost as long as hers. Kate's got her kitten in her lap, and Elly's holding on to Bek's hand tightly even as she sits. I wish I had a kitten—or a kid—in my lap. Something to do with my hands to get rid of all this nervous energy.

Of course, then Warrek brushes a hand against my hair, and I start thinking of dirtier things to do with my hands. Not the time, Summer. Not. The. Time.

"She is with kit," Vektal says, touching his chest. "We have resonated for a third time."

"That's wonderful!" Gail exclaims, and a few others murmur their agreement. Seems weird to be celebrating when the look on Vektal's face is so solemn.

"Does she normally faint?" I blurt out. "Or is that our fault because we're the bearers of bad news? I mean, not that we could sit on the news and just not share it—that'd be an even bigger dick move. I guess there's no good way to bring up a tribe-changing event, but you know what I mean. I'd feel guilty if her conking out was a result of us—"

"Yes and no," Vektal says, interrupting my verbal stream. Thank god. I can't seem to stop myself lately. "This kit has been harder on her stomach than the last. She is not eating as she should." He rubs a hand down his face, looking stressed. "And she worries over all of the humans in the tribe. She feels responsible for you, like a mother with a kit. The thought of twenty new humans overwhelmed her."

"Sixteen," I add helpfully.

Warrek's fingers brush against my neck, and he tweaks my earlobe. Right. I should probably shut up. I cringe a half-smile at Vektal when he looks in my direction, frowning.

"The good news is that our tribesmates are safe," Warrek says in his calm, smooth voice. "No one was injured by the slavers. And they have all been dealt with."

Vektal scrubs his hand down his face again and nods. "That is good. That is very good. Tell me what happened."

There's a pause, and then Bek begins to speak. He talks of the landing of the ship and how everyone rushed out to greet them. It wasn't until they were halfway down the ramp that the sa-khui realized they weren't friendly, and then it was too late. They captured the men and women and separated them in individual cells, except for Taushen and Brooke, whom they threw together. Bek then goes on to tell of our guns-blazing rescue, supplied with missing details by Warrek's quiet additions to the story. Eventually he gets to the part about opening the boxes and revealing all the sleeping humans.

I kind of expect him to comment about that, but Vektal just looks troubled. "I do not like that Rukh and Farli and the others are so far away. If enemies were to come again, our kin are many days away from even the fastest of hunters. I would rather them be here, where we can aid them."

"They work on the ship," Harrec says. "Important work, Mardok says."

Vektal just strokes his chin thoughtfully. "Important to Mardok and Har-loh perhaps, but would it be safer to give up on the Elders' Caves and live as we do? Do we need their speaking machines? Or the healing machine, when we have Maylak's gentle hands?"

"We should get rid of it," Bek says fiercely, and I'm startled at the vehemence in his tone. "The slavers said they followed a trail left by Trakan and the others to our home world. What if others come looking for the ship and attack us again? We must bury it. Find a deep valley, bury it in snow, hide it from everything."

"But the technology," Kate protests. "It could help us, especially with Mardok and Harlow working together—"

"Not if it brings more of those orange strangers to our world," Bek growls at her, clearly on edge.

"Do not threaten my mate," Harrec snaps, pushing between the seated Kate and the hovering Bek. Elly just squeezes Bek's hand, reminding him to calm down, and he backs off.

"Enough," Vektal says, raising a hand. "There are many layers to this that must be discussed. I do not deny that we would be losing much by destroying the home of our ancestors. But like Bek, I worry that the new ship will bring others here."

"And as we saw when they arrived, they have light-spears and we have bone spears," Vaza says, arms crossed. "We are no match for that sort of thing."

Gail smooths Rukhar's hair down his head. "You know, I bet Rukhar's tired. Why don't we go see if Stacy's got some not-potato cakes cooking?" She gives all of us a warning look and pats Rukhar's shoulder. They get up, and she takes his hand, leading him out of the circle and down the steps of the longhouse into the village.

"Har-loh and Rukh were wise to send him back," Vektal says after a moment. "He is safer here. That is what concerns me. If Har-loh, who loves the ships and ma-sheens, feels they are not safe, then are they safe for anyone? Or must we do as Bek says and destroy them so others do not follow them to us?"

"The people," Elly whispers, her voice so low my ears strain to catch it. "What of them?"

Vektal sighs heavily, and he looks tired. "I do not know."

"We can't just leave them," Kate protests.

"The return of the other aliens has made me realize," Vektal says, choosing each word carefully, "that just because someone arrives at our home, it does not mean they are friendly. We must be cautious. We do not know that these others will blend in with our family."

"You made us blend," I protest. When everyone turns to look at me, I add, "I don't mean it badly. I mean that we came here, and we weren't exactly thrilled to be on an ice planet, but the people were nice, and it worked out."

"Five is easier to blend with a tribe than twenty," Bek says. "I agree that they might be dangerous." He holds Elly's hand tightly. "We do not want to endanger those that already live here."

"We can't just leave them, either," Kate protests. "That seems wrong."

It seems wrong to me, too.

"I do not have an answer," Vektal says. He seems tired, as if the weight of responsibility for twenty more people is already weighing on his shoulders. "I will talk with my mate and we will discuss with others. We need to consider this from all sides. What if we awaken them and they are the enemy? What if they are not slaves at all?"

"What if they are and need to be rescued?" I blurt. "What if they're stolen like we were?"

Vektal nods at me. "And then there is that. With the exception of Taushen, Warrek, and Sessah, all our males are mated, too old to resonate, or kits. There are four males in the group, but that does not mean they will resonate. We do not have enough mates for everyone."

"Dude, not everyone needs a man in their life," I blurt again. "That's total caveman thinking."

Warrek leans over me, his silky hair falling against my shoulder. "I think my chief means that it is unfair to them to put them in a tribe where there is no one to help them."

"That, and I do not have the males to mate them," Vektal says.

"See?" I whisper to Warrek. "Caveman."

"I must think of the happiness of the tribe. Will they be happy if they are unable to have mates? To be permanently alone? Or is that selfish of me to assume?"

"Can I answer that one?" I ask, raising my hand. I'm a little annoyed at this line of thinking. Like we need a man to make our hearts happy? For real?

"Do not," Warrek murmurs, leaning over me again. He tweaks my earlobe, and it sends a shiver up my spine.

Okay, maybe I don't need a man, but having the company of one sure helps. Maybe he's right and that seeing a bunch of happy fur-wearing mommies and daddies wandering around and smooching on each other might make the others cranky and malcontent. I know I've had my moments, envying the others.

"There is much to consider," Vektal says, getting to his feet. "I must go speak to my Georgie. All of you, rest for the evening. Relax. I will speak with you again one-on-one as the need arises." He moves forward and clasps Warrek on the arm, then Vaza. "But I am glad you are all safe. That is more important than anything."

"And we must stay safe," Bek adds, both of his hands on Elly's shoulders. "I do not care if we sacrifice the Elders' Cave. Or the new one. All I care about is the safety of my mate and my kit."

"I think like you," Vektal says with a nod. His face looks grim. "But I must think of all my people before I make a decision."

15

WARREK

*a*s the healer fusses over me, I think about Vektal. My chief looks grimmer than I have ever seen him. Over the seasons, as our tribe has grown, his high-spirited smiles have given way to thoughtful glances, and I know he and his mate Shorshie worry over all of us. It is clear that leadership is a mantle that weighs heavily upon Vektal's shoulders.

I am glad it is his shoulders and not mine.

The tribe is celebrating our return, and with the evening, a large fire is built at the front of the longhouse. Harrec stands near it, gesturing with wild hands and telling the story of Suh-mer's courageous rescue as Stay-see cooks her treats for everyone. Suh-mer's courageous rescue, I mull. I think of it as *her* rescue of the others, not mine. She was the one with the ideas, the plans, the daring. The chess. I was simply her helper. I look for my small, brave mate, but I do not see her by the fire. Kate is there, beaming up at her new mate, and her small snow-cat is being petted by every kit gathered near the fire. The little animal is patient, at least, and appears to enjoy the attention. Who knew the ferocious creatures could be so affectionate?

There is a thread of worry for those still at the ship, and I have watched others move to the chief's side to speak to him more than once this day. With every conversation, his face seems a little more lined, a little more tired.

It is not easy being chief, and I worry it will be too much for him and Shorshie at some point. No doubt it was easier when there were only ten or twelve hands of us. Now there are kits everywhere, more on the way, and people have been counting the empty houses at the edge of the village, thinking of where the newcomers will live. It is a lot of mouths to keep fed.

I think of the houses, the small, stone huts that were here long before we arrived. There are yet several that can be fixed up, ready for new couples. Harrec and Kate will be occupying one, I think, now that they are mated. Shail and Vaza will move in together as well. That leaves Suh-mer and Buh-brukh alone in their hut, and myself, Taushen and Sessah in the hunters' hut.

I wonder if Suh-mer will share furs with me permanently, if I ask? I already think of her as mine, but she might have different ideas. She might wish to wait for resonance. The thought is a startling one, and even more startling is the jealous surge that rushes through me. I am a calm hunter. I do not let things bother me.

But the idea of another male—Taushen or Sessah—touching my Suh-mer? It makes me growl and bare my teeth at the night.

"You are well enough," Maylak says, lifting her hands from my shoulder. "Your khui is strong and bold yet."

I nod. I knew this to be the case. I was not harmed by the aliens, nor did I injure myself in the rescue of the others, but Maylak still insisted upon checking me over. It is the mother in her, I suppose, because I have no family left to care for me.

I think of Suh-mer. She would fuss over my wounds, I think, and the thought makes me smile to myself. I imagine her endless chatter as she bathes a minor wound, and the thought of her hands on me makes my cock harden. She has wanted to put her hands on me for days now, but I have distracted her from such things. We did not have the time.

Now, it seems, we have all the time we could possibly want.

Maylak gives me a little pat. "If you see Ell-ee, send her to me. I think Bek is hiding her away."

"He will bring her to you, I imagine." The overprotective hunter would not wish any harm to come to his fragile mate. "But I shall look for them."

"My thanks. You can go rejoin the others now." She indicates the emptying group near the bonfire, where a few have trickled away to put their kits to sleep. Others remain, and the skins of sah-sah are being passed around. I glance at Vektal again. He does not drink and wears a distant expression. The newcomers weigh on him heavily.

"Have you seen Suh-mer?" I ask, because I do not see her near the bonfire with the others.

"Mmm, she was here earlier." She gives a little shrug and yawns. "Her khui is a strong one."

As it should be. My female is fierce and brave. "My thanks." I get to my feet, stretching, and then head toward the bonfire. Perhaps one of the others there knows where she has gone.

But on the way to the bonfire, I see Bek and his mate emerging from the chief's hut. I pause and speak to them, indicating that they should visit the healer, and Bek tells me that he was visiting Shorshie, who is still in her furs, sick to her stomach. He wants her to convince Vektal that destroying the ships will protect us all. And he wants me to speak to Shorshie about this as well.

"The more voices, the better," he says, his arm around Ell-ee's shoulders. She leans against him, her eyes haunted, and I feel a stab of pity for her. Out of all the humans, she seems the most damaged by her experiences. Perhaps that is why Bek is so fiercely protective. I think of Suh-mer and the way she grabbed the light-spear and charged forward, killing her attackers. Is she brave and bold because she was not held captive as long as Ell-ee? Or is she just brave and bold because that is who she is?

"Warrek?" Bek snaps. "Did you hear me?"

"My thoughts were elsewhere," I admit. "But I will speak to Shorshie when I have made up my mind about the ships."

"The humans are not safe as long as they exist," Bek exclaims. "What part of that do you not grasp?"

"I do not wish to make a hasty judgment," I tell him. Even as I do, I pause. I think of Suh-mer. She handled herself well against the enemy, but I remember her burned face and blistered fingers. I think of her eyebrows that were singed off. She had not even realized she was hurt. She acts as she speaks—immediately and without cautious thought.

It would be very easy for another to take advantage of that, to entrap her and enslave her once more. I think of Suh-mer and her bright smile, her endless stream of words. I think of her clever mind. I think of her as broken as Ell-ee once was, covered in dirt, a hunted expression on her face.

The thought makes my gut churn. "I shall speak to Shorshie in the morning."

Bek nods at me, pleased. "It is a wise move."

I do not know if it is a wise move, but it is what I will do. If Mardok and Har-loh must be disappointed in the loss of the ships, I find it does not matter to me as much as Suh-mer's safety. I will tell Suh-mer my decision, wait to see what she says, and then I will speak to Shorshie in the morning. "Take your mate to the healer," I tell Bek. "I must find Suh-mer."

"Be ready for tomorrow," he tells me as I step away.

I turn back to him, frowning. "What is tomorrow?"

"If Vektal wishes to go to the ships, we will likely leave right away. He will need many strong hunters with him, especially if we are to bring the humans back to the tribe with us."

I ponder this. It is not something I considered, and yet it makes sense. If we need to move to protect the tribe, we must do so immediately. I do not like the thought of leaving Suh-mer, but I like the thought of her being captured even less. It must be done. I nod at him. "I will be ready."

For now, though, I wish to be with Suh-mer.

16

WARREK

I head back toward the fire.

When I arrive, I look for Shail. She shares quarters with Suh-mer. She will know where she is at. But Shail is gone with Vaza and Rukhar. Kate sits near the fire, her snow-cat in her lap, watching her mate with shining eyes. She gives a nervous giggle. Nearby, several of the mated hunters are watching Harrec with open skepticism.

"There he is!" Harrec points at me. "Warrek, come. I have been telling them about your discovery and they do not believe me."

Wary, I move forward, joining the others. Haeden scowls at me as I approach, Salukh, Erevan, and Rokan his audience. Mah-dee stands with Hassen's arm around her shoulders, and she has an amused look on her face.

"I am telling them of the she-spot," Harrec mock-whispers at me. "They do not believe me."

Ah. I shrug, glancing around at the edges of the fire in case Suh-mer wanders near. "My female told me of it. She said it was a pleasure spot for humans."

"That is the third nipple," Haeden says, clearly displeased.

"There is another," I tell him. "The she-spot."

Haeden grunts, skeptical.

"I wish to know more," Ereven says, a grin on his face. "Anything to please my Claire."

"Does this truly work?" Salukh asks.

"Oh yeah," Kate says dreamily. She gets a funny look on her face and focuses on petting her snow-cat.

"It does work," Mah-dee adds, a little smile on her mouth. "And it's not that much of a secret. Hassen has always found my G-spot."

"I have?" Hassen seems clearly surprised by this.

Mah-dee crooks a finger and Hassen leans in. She whispers at him, and then he chuckles.

"Ah, that spot. Yes." He grins, pleased.

"Tell us," Haeden demands, turning to me. "I wish to know more about this."

I clap a hand on Harrec's shoulder. "You tell them. I must find Suh-mer."

"And her she-spot?" Harrec teases.

Salukh leans forward and taps on Harrec's shoulder. "Focus. Tell us about this spot."

I head away before I can be trapped into a story. Kate's high-pitched, nervous-but-pleased giggles follow me into the night.

All I want to find is Suh-mer. As the day wears on, I find that I crave her company more and more. Already I miss her presence at my side. Is this how it will be now that we have returned to the village? If so, I do not like it. I see now why others have dragged their mates away from the tribe to spend time privately with them. It is tempting to do so, but for now, I must remain. The tribe is in turmoil with the discovery of twenty newcomers, and every hunter will be needed.

But it does not mean I do not think about it. A lot.

Suh-mer is not in her hut. The privacy screen is up, but there is no fire lit inside, and it is too cold a night to go without. She is somewhere else, then. The need to see her fills me with longing. She must be here somewhere. I will search every hut if I must, but I need to hear her voice and see her smile.

The craving to see her, the need to know she is safe, intensifies with every step I take through the village. When I finally find her in one of the empty huts, pushing aside storage baskets, I feel a sense of overwhelming relief. I do not know why I am reacting so strongly to the thought of her leaving my side, but I cannot shake the possessiveness I feel. She is *mine.*

It will be difficult to leave her behind to go with Vektal and his band of hunters, I realize as I watch her slight form move in the darkness. Who will look after her when she charges ahead? Who will make her calm when her mind—and her mouth—are full of worries?

I had hoped to make a chessboard with her, to talk more of the game she loves so much. Now it must wait, just like everything else. I feel a stab of resentment, which is surprising for me. I do not try to let many things get under my skin, but the thought of leaving Suh-mer makes me want to snarl.

I am becoming just like Bek.

She turns, and at the sight of me in the shadows nearby, gives a small, startled scream and jumps. "Oh my god! You scared the shit out of me, Warrek! Why are you lurking?" She collapses to her knees and puts a hand to her chest. "If you wanted to say hello, you should have done so. Is something else wrong? Or is there a problem? Is someone looking for me?"

Her stream of quick, flurrying questions is comforting. I step forward and take the basket from her hands. "I was looking for you. What are you doing here?"

"Oh." She pushes her mane back and takes a deep breath. "Well, between Gail and Vaza hooking up, and Kate and Harrec, I figured someone is going to claim the hut. I mean, I guess I could stay, but the thought of sleeping there while they're all making out isn't my favorite. I know we did a little heavy petting by the fire and all, but I suspect they're going to be doing more than petting. And really, new couples deserve their privacy. So I thought I'd see if I could move into one of these huts with minimal fuss. This one has a nice roof on it, and I don't mind sleeping next to baskets, but I need a spot to put my bed and maybe a fire pit and—" She glances around, sighing. "I didn't think it'd be much work, but now that I'm in the weeds, it feels like a ton."

"I will help," I tell her, moving the basket to the far side of the small hut. This one is heavily decorated with the carvings of the tribe that lived here long ago. Pictures etched in stone cover the walls, and I gaze at the strange, four-armed people in the carvings for a moment. Were they taken by the orange-skinned strangers, I wonder? Is that why they are all gone? The uneasiness grows in the pit of my stomach, and now, more than ever, I have to fight the urge not to leave Suh-mer behind.

But I must go with my chief. He will need all the hunters with him, and I do not have any kits or a mate to provide for.

"You're so sweet," Suh-mer is saying happily, as if unaware that I am moments away from tearing off my tunic and throwing myself atop her. "But maybe I'll just put up with the grunting for a day or two. I don't think I'll be sleeping here tonight. It's a little cold, and I'm not good with fire...though I suppose I could always just steal a coal or two from the main fire pit. That might work." She dusts her hands off on her tunic. "I'll be right back. I'll go grab a coal and work on the fire, and maybe we can get things started here. I really do appreciate the help. You're nice to offer, Warrek. I know you have to be tired, and I'm sure you've got things to do."

She moves to step past me, and I put a hand on her shoulder, stopping her. "No fire," I decide. "I will be the one that keeps you warm tonight."

"Oh?" A husky note enters her voice.

"Tonight and every night," I decide firmly. "You are my female, and I will be your hunter. You and I will have a hut together, and we will play chess and hunt and mate in the furs every night."

She gets a flustered look on her face. "Um, so that sounds okay to me. But will anyone care if we claim a hut together?"

"I do not care if they do." I put my arms around her, caressing her cheek. "We shall be pleasure-mates in all ways."

"Well, since it's all decided," she says breathlessly, and then chuckles. "For a quiet guy, you sure are decisive."

"I know what I want," I tell her. "That has never wavered. I have wanted you ever since you spoke of chess." I pull on the tie at the neck of her tunic. "And since you have taught me about chess, I have decided that I am going to use such a strategy to get my female in my furs."

"You are?"

I nod. "Right now, I am taking my opponent off-guard. Soon I shall rush into her territory."

"Sounds dirty."

Does it? I like the thought. I tug the neck of her tunic open a bit more, revealing the curves of her teats. She is beautiful in the moonlight, and I want to tell her such things. To give her the words she always gives me, but I have none. "If I were to play chess," I murmur, "what would be my next move?"

"Against me?" She slides a hand up my stomach, raking her fingernails across my abdomen, and shivering. "I'd tell you to capture my pawns."

Her pawns? The small pieces that have maneuverability? I slide a hand into the front of her tunic, cupping one teat and teasing her nipple. "And then?"

Suh-mer sighs, a look of longing on her face. "I'd tell you to take my queen. It's been waiting ever so long."

I groan, bending to kiss her. Our mouths slick together, and the taste of her fills my senses. Nothing has ever brought me more pleasure than putting my lips on Suh-mer. It does not matter where—her mouth, her cunt, her soft skin—all of her makes my mouth water with need. "Tonight is our night," I promise her. "No one will interrupt. No one will tell us to hurry to our furs. No one will be near. It will be you and me and no one else around. We will mate as we should." I drag my thumb over her nipple. "And we will take our time."

She shivers, watching me with luminous eyes. "I like that thought."

The wind rips through the hut, blowing my hair around us, and she shivers again. I am a fool, I realize as she steps closer, letting my body block the night breeze. She shivers from desire, yes, but also from cold. There are no furs in this storage hut, no fire. If I were to take her now, it would be on the hard-packed stone floor.

I can do better for the female that has my heart.

Reluctantly, I slide my hand out of her tunic and cup her chin. I kiss her mouth, hard and firm, my tongue stroking against hers in that possessive, determined way that always makes her moan. "Wait here," I tell her when I break the kiss. "I will build us a fire."

Her eyes brighten, and she nods at me, tugging her tunic closed. "I'll clear a bit more of the floor while you do that."

My lovely mate. My cock aches, and I want to fling my leathers off and just pull her against me, but I want this to be perfect for her. I must learn to be more patient.

At least, more patient in some things. In others, I do not think haste is a bad idea. I exit the hut and then race across the village to the hut at the outskirts that the hunters share. My things are there: my furs, my weapons, my extra clothes. I grab my tunics, my supplies bag in case she wishes to eat or drink, and then fill my arms with my furs.

Sessah enters, lanky arms and long legs folding onto his furs. "What is it you do, Warrek?"

"I am going to share a hut with Suh-mer," I tell him. "She is mine."

He looks surprised. "You resonated, too?"

I shake my head. "No. It does not matter, though. I have claimed her, and she has claimed me."

"Mmm." He folds his legs under him and watches me gather my furs. "Is it true? That there are many females in the second ship?"

"Sixteen," I agree.

"Pretty? My age?"

I shrug. Or try to. I have so much gear in my arms I cannot see where I walk. I know the hut though, and where the door is. "I have eyes for none but Suh-mer."

"Bah," Sessah says. "Maybe I will join the others and get myself a mate. See which of the newcomers resonates for me."

"Do that," I tell him, and waddle out the door with my belongings. I hesitate a moment and then grab the privacy screen from the front of the hut and drag it along with me.

"Hey!" Sessah calls. "What are you doing?"

"You do not need privacy this night," I yell behind me. "I do."

He grumbles something that is lost to the wind.

17

WARREK

I manage to make my way to Suh-mer's hut without dropping any of the gear overflowing my arms, a small feat in itself. Once there, I drop my burdens and glance around the hut. Suh-mer has cleared a large portion of the floor. Baskets are stacked atop one another in the corner, and supplies have been lumped together instead of spread out. There is room for a fire pit and for us to stretch out in the furs. She has been hard at work, and I am pleased. Suh-mer is not one to sit around and wait for others to do things for her. She is full of action; it is another thing I like about her.

She is also hugging her arms and doing a little half-dance that tells me she is very cold. I pick up one of the furs and move to her, draping it around her shoulders. "I will make you a fire."

"I would love a fire." She beams up at me.

Then I shall make it the best, warmest fire I have ever created, I decide. And the quickest, because I do not wish for my mate to suffer from the cold any longer than she must. She is mine to care for, and I want everything to be perfect for her. I drop to my knees and begin placing the gathered stones in a ring to capture the ash, then pull out my fire bundle and begin to build a fire.

"I guess I can make the bed," Suh-mer says breathlessly, jumping to her feet. "It'll probably be good for me to keep busy while you do that, because I'm getting all nervous, and I know I shouldn't be, but I am." She gives a little laugh at her own words. "I guess because we've been anticipating this for a while, right? Or at least, I have. And now that it's finally here, I'm all jittery at the thought. It's silly, of course, because we've touched each other in all kinds of ways. But this just feels..."

"Bigger," I agree, not looking up from my work.

"Yes. Bigger." She shakes out the furs at the far side of the hut. "And I guess everyone's going to know what we're up to the moment they see we've claimed a place of our own. I probably shouldn't care about that, but it makes me blush. I suppose that's normal, though. All newlyweds go through that kind of thing. Not that we're newlyweds," she adds quickly. "I don't want you to think that I'm making this out to be more than it is. We're just hooking up, right? Right. So if things don't go the way we want, no harm done either way. We're both consenting adults."

She talks with great speed, and I sit up, frowning. She is very nervous. To be with me? I do not understand why. "What is this 'noo-lee-wed'?" I ask.

"Oh, um, it's nothing. Just a term humans use." Her words are quick.

I wait. When she does not offer, I add, "If it is nothing, then say what it is."

Suh-mer takes great interest in smoothing a fur blanket. "It's, you know…"

"I do not." Her reluctance to speak of it worries me.

She makes an exasperated sound and then blurts out the rest. "It's when humans decide to get married. Newly married people are called newlyweds. Married's like being mated. But I know we're not mated, so—"

"We are," I tell her calmly. "Do not worry."

"We are?" She looks astounded. "Since when?"

"Since I have decided."

"Dude, you can't just decide that! What about, you know," She drops her voice. "Cooties?"

She uses the human word for khui. "If one of us resonates, we shall deal with it then. I will not live the rest of my days waiting for it to happen. I wish to be with no other than the one that holds my heart."

"That's me?" she whispers.

"Of course it is." I bend low to blow on the fire.

Suh-mer gives a happy squeal, and in the next moment, I feel her arms go around my neck, and her light body clings to my back. "Oh my god! I love you, too, Warrek! Why didn't you just say so? I've been stewing for hours wondering if we were done now that we were home! I didn't know what to think!"

"Why? What has changed?" I pat her arm, turning my head so I can rub my nose against hers. Or try to, anyhow.

"Everything? Nothing? I mean, we're back at the village. I thought maybe it was just a travel booty-call sort of thing. Not that you're the type to do a booty call, but I didn't know what to think when we got back and you disappeared on me."

"I had to talk to the chief." I stroke her soft, soft arms. "Let me finish building this fire and I will show you how much you mean to me."

"Oh boy, why does that sound so sweet and yet so dirty?" She slides off my back and saunters over to the furs, taking off her boots. "Can I get naked?"

"The thought pleases me very much," I tell her, and fight the urge to adjust my cock in my loincloth. Fire first. Warm my mate, then warm her with my body.

I feed tinder to the tiny flame, making it grow. As I do, Suh-mer hums a tune to herself, and when I glance over, I realize she is under the blankets, undressing. My cock aches harder, and I feel my sac tighten as I imagine her golden skin brushing against the soft fur. She wiggles under the blankets and then tosses her tunic into the corner of the hut. "Oh, I just realized we didn't put the privacy screen over the door," Suh-mer tells me. She gets to her feet, fur wrapped around her body, and I realize she is naked underneath. I could peel the furs off of her and bare her cunt for my mouth within a flash.

Mine. My mate.

The ferocious, possessive feeling surges inside me once more.

No other male will ever touch her. Not one of the newcomers. Not Taushen. Not Sessah. It does not matter that we have not resonated. She is mine.

She places the privacy screen over the entrance and wedges it taut in the doorway. I take a bit of leather and use it to grab a couple of dung-cakes, dropping them onto the fire. I am careful not to touch them—I do not want to handle dung and then touch my female. When the fire is blazing warmth, I sit up and glance around. She is still by the entrance, holding the furs to her teats. As I look over, she smiles—

—And drops the furs.

Her naked body is lovely. Bare skin is nothing new to a sa-khui. As a people, we are not ashamed of nudity, and I have seen many of the tribe—both human and otherwise—completely unclothed. It is different for humans, though, and many are shy to reveal themselves. Suh-mer is one of them. Each time I see her bare, it steals the breath from my body. She is delicate and lithe, her form perfect, her teats small and high. She saunters back to the bed, swaying her bottom as she walks past me. It is lovely— all rounded and golden and without a hint of a tail. As always, I am fascinated by the sight of it.

She bends over at the waist, leaning over the furs, and as she does, I see a hint of her cunt peeking through the cleft of her bottom as she bends over. Her teats bounce as she leans, and I do not know what I want to touch first. I want to put my mouth on all of her. "You tease me," I breathe.

"Yup. You like it?" She wiggles her bottom at me.

I growl low in my throat. Do I like it? I hunger for it—and for her.

But I do not answer her; I will show her instead. I grab her by the hips and haul her backward. She squeals and flails her arms, trying to catch her balance. After a moment, she topples into my lap, a sprawl of limbs and flying, shiny mane. Her teats bounce as she gasps, eyes wide. "Warrek!"

"Shall I show you how much I like it?"

"Yes, please," she breathes, a smile widening across her face. "You don't have to ask me twice."

I get to my feet and carry her back to the furs. Even as I do, she toys with the long strands of my mane, dragging the ends over her skin and teasing her nipples with it. The sight is a fascinating one, and I'm torn by the desire to watch her endlessly or to touch her myself.

The need to touch her wins out, though. I lay her down gently in the furs and nip the budded tip of one teat.

Suh-mer moans, stretching her arms over her head and thrusting them higher. "I thought you were going to go for my butt."

"In time," I tell her, giving her nipple a lick. "I am going to taste all of you this night."

She gives a happy little sigh at the thought. "Mmm, I like that."

I do, as well. I run my fingers through her shiny mane, spreading it out on the furs around her head like a halo. She has no horns, and while at first I found it strange, now I enjoy that she seems so small and different. I like her differences. They fascinate me and arouse my senses. Her expressions are far more intense than any sa-khui female's would be; when she is surprised, her brow goes up, and when she is angry, her brow goes down. It does not matter that her eyebrows are gone. It is still easy to tell which touches please her and which do not. She cannot keep it to herself, and it makes it easy to read her.

Like right now. Her hands have gone to my mane once more, and she is watching me with the softest expression, even as she pulls my mane forward and spreads it over my shoulders like a cape. "You're so pretty," she sighs dreamily. "And you have the best hair of any guy here."

"I do, eh?" I nip her breast again, unable to resist.

"You do."

"And my horns?"

Her little brow furrows. "They're, um, horny? Big and horny?"

I chuckle at the description. "You do not find my horns erotic?"

"Should I?" A worried look crosses her face. "I mean, they're great horns, and I'm not trying to insult. I just like your hair so much better. Not that you would look better without horns. I think you look great with them. I'm just not used to judging horns, and I don't know what a good horn looks like compared to a bad horn, and I'm babbling, aren't I?" She gives me a chagrined smile.

"You are." I lean in to kiss her lightly. "But I do not mind it."

"You're the only one," she mutters. "Most people get tired of it pretty damn fast, especially when I put my foot in my mouth, as I tend to do repeatedly."

"I am not most people," I tell her with a lick to her navel. She shivers and sucks in as I do so, and it makes me want to taste her there again. "And I like your talking. You can talk as much as you want around me, and I will enjoy all of it."

Suh-mer sighs happily. "And that's why you're the best guy ever. I never feel like you're just waiting for me to shut up."

"If you were silent, I would miss your thoughts," I admit, kissing lower. Her skin is exceptionally soft here.

"Are you sure you're not crazy? Because I think you're the only man in the world that would say that." Her hands stray to my horns, and she holds the base of one tightly as I move lower. She sighs deeply as I nuzzle the tuft of hair over her mound. "If we're going to take our sweet time, should I point out that you're going directly to third base? I don't mind it—I actually love third base —but I thought perhaps I should mention it."

I do not know what this "third base" is. "I like your cunt," I tell her. "And I like licking it. I see no problem with going directly to it."

"Oh boy, I like it when you lick it, too," she breathes, and her hand tightens on my horn. "I'm gonna shut up now. Carry on."

I chuckle and give her a long, slow taste. My groan of bliss is drowned out in her cry of pleasure, and she squirms underneath me. I love how she responds, and it fills me with fierce, possessive need. I want to do more. I want to see her arch underneath me, mouth parted as she comes hard. I want to feel her cunt clench around my finger. More than that, I want to sink into her and feel her warmth clasp my cock. I want to fill her with my seed and surge deep into her body. I am hungry to claim all of her.

I let hunger drive my tongue. Each lick, each drag of the tip of my tongue over her cunt, is filled with the intensity rushing through me. I need her, and I have waited long enough. Tonight, she is mine.

"Oh!" Suh-mer cries as I circle her clit like she has shown me. "Oh god, that's really good." Her hands go behind her head, and she clasps the blankets tight. Her legs hook over my shoulders, and I can feel her thighs squeezing against my ears. "You're going to kill me with your tongue. You really, really are. Oh god. Oh shit. Oh, Warrek."

I punctuate her words with a lick each time. My cock is surging fiercely in my loincloth, and I yearn to take my leathers off and press my skin to hers. Perhaps I want too much, too quickly.

But then she moans again, and I taste fresh wetness on her cunt, and my senses are inflamed once more. No waiting, no longer. She is mine, and with every soft cry of my name, she makes it more difficult to resist.

I want her to come first, I think. At least once before I bury myself inside her. I know from our previous pleasurings that she can come quickly if I touch her just right. So I continue to flick my tongue against her clit even as I press a finger to the entrance of her core. She is hot and slick here, and I ease my finger into her. Her cunt is tight, but the feeling is indescribable. My sac tightens against my cock, and it takes all of my control not to come at once. I grind my hips against the furs as she clenches around my finger. I can now find her she-spot easily, but I wish to tease her a little. I drag my fingertip over it and then thrust into her.

Suh-mer cries out, her thighs clenching my face.

I slide my finger out of her and then thrust in again, enjoying her reaction. When I thrust into her again, I add a second finger, stretching her. My cock is much bigger than my fingers, so I must make her ready to take me.

"Tongue," she pants. "Need more tongue, Warrek. I'm so close." She rocks down on my fingers, trying to push me deeper into her. "Need more everything."

I give her a long, slow, teasing lick. "Does your queen require more...strategy?"

"Warrek, hon, I love you," she pants. "But that makes no sense. Your queen needs you to stick your big bishop into her. No, wait, a king. Your dick is definitely a king." She bites down on her lip. "And now I'm using the terrible chess metaphors. Don't care. I just need to *come*."

There is an insistent edge in her voice, and I realize she is close. I angle my fingers again, making sure to stroke against her she-spot inside her when I thrust. Her choked scream tells me this is what she needs, and I suck lightly on her clit to increase her pleasure.

Her cry as she comes is ear-shattering, and I cannot stop the fierce smile that curves my face. Let them all hear my female come as I pleasure her. I continue to pump into her, making her release last as long as possible. She shudders and falls back onto the furs, limp and panting.

Satisfied that she has enjoyed herself, I get to my feet and begin to strip off my leathers.

Suh-mer opens her eyes and watches me. "Go slower."

"Eh?" I pause, curious.

She sits up on her elbows, a tiny smile curving her mouth. "I wanted to watch the show. Go slower. Let me enjoy the unwrapping. I haven't gotten to see much, you know. There's never been time."

I realize she is right. In all of our furtive pleasurings, she has not had the opportunity to take my leathers off. Her hands have moved over my cock through the leather, but other than that, it has been all about her. Now she wants me to undress slowly to please her? I like the thought, but I also want to be on top of her, sinking into her.

When I hesitate, she wiggles her brow at me. "Don't be shy. I'm sure you don't have anything I haven't seen before."

She thinks I am shy? I chuckle and undo the knots at my leather loincloth, letting it and my leggings drop to the floor.

Suh-mer makes a sound of protest. "You were supposed to do that slow!" Her eyes widen and she stares at my cock.

"What is it?"

"I forgot," she whispers. "You *do* have something I haven't seen before."

I stroke a hand down my length. It feels good, but not as good as being seated inside her would feel. "What is wrong?"

"Nothing's wrong! I just..." She has an embarrassed look on her face. "Sorta forgot about the spur. I'm sure it's fine, though. If it was a problem, I imagine someone would have said something earlier. And Gail did try to warn me. I just forgot, is all. Looks nice. I mean, not that the rest of you doesn't look nice, but I'm just being polite. I'm sure it's a very nice spur." Her words creep together, faster and faster. "Not that your dick isn't nice, too—"

"Hush," I tell her, and gesture at my cock. "Do you wish to touch me and learn me with your hands?"

Her lips part, and then she nods, an eager expression on her face. "Would you mind?"

"If my mate touched me? Never." Just the thought has my cock aching. As I glance down, I see fresh pre-cum glide down the head of my cock.

She sits up on her knees, one hand going to my thigh. "Do you need a moment?"

I shake my head. I can control myself. I hope. I close my eyes, because the thought of watching her explore me makes me want to push her into the furs and claim my release. I must be patient.

"All right, then." Her voice is soft and her hand hesitant on my thigh. "Just say something if I do or touch something you don't like."

I nod. What else is there to say? My entire body is tense with anticipation. I remain utterly still, waiting for those first touches.

Even so, I am still not prepared. A hand gently touches my sac, and she cups it in her palms, her fingers teasing my skin. The breath explodes out of me, and I groan. My hands clench at my sides, curled into fists so I do not grab her and scare her. The need I feel for her is dangerously close to blazing out of control, though.

"Your skin is soft here, and it feels hotter than the rest of you. Is that my imagination?" She presses something to my thigh. Her cheek? Her teat? "No, I guess you're the same warmth everywhere. Maybe it just feels different because it's so close to your thighs." Her fingers stroke my sac lightly. "Feels different than how I imagined. Does this feel good?"

All I can manage is a jerky nod. "Everything you do feels good, my mate."

"Your mate? I like that. I think that's definitely better than 'newlywed.'" She chuckles at the thought. "But I suppose if we were newlyweds, this would be our honeymoon. That's a little trip that a newly married couple takes to get away from everyone so they can just enjoy being married. Kind of a celebration of the union."

"Like when the others kidnapped their mates when they resonated," I agreed.

"Not *quite* the same thing, but you're getting warmer." Her hands leave my sac and land on my thighs again. "Is it okay if I touch your cock? You look a little stressed. Are you going to blow your wad? Do I need to stop?"

18

WARREK

*H*er stream of questions is difficult to concentrate on when all I can think of is how her hands feel on my thigh and where she will put them next. "Touch me how you like," I manage to grit out.

"Okay, but the moment I see a hint of an O-face, I'm pulling back."

I am about to agree with her strange words when she lightly strokes my shaft.

Then, it is impossible to think of anything. I am lost to the sensation of her delicate fingers dancing against my skin, the murmurs of appreciation she makes as she explores me, the soft fan of her breath against my flesh. "Ridges here, too. Sweet lord have mercy. And it feels like your skin is even hotter here. Wow. And you're big, too. I mean, I knew you'd be big, but...this seems big." Her fingers squeeze the underside of my cockhead. "Can't-quite-get-my-fingers-around-you big. Not that I'm an expert on big, but seeing up close and personal, it's a little intimidating."

I grunt, because I do not wish to influence her. Let her touch me as she likes; I will enjoy all of it.

"Is your spur sensitive?" she asks, whispering. Her fingers graze the length of it, and I am about to tell her no when she strokes the underside. That small brush of her fingers sends a shudder rippling through my body, and I have to bite back my groan of response.

"I'm thinking that's a yes." Suh-mer flutters her hands over my length again. "There's so much here, and you're so...gorgeous. I think I might need to give myself a moment."

"Take what you need," I manage thickly.

"If you say so." Her tone is suddenly playful, and in the next moment, her mouth is closing over the head of my cock. The breath leaves my body as she flicks her tongue against my skin and then swirls it, over and over. Suh-mer makes a small noise of pleasure as she does. Her hand curls against my shaft, as if feeding it to her.

And then I have to look. I will die if I do not.

The sight of her sucking on my cock is the most incredible thing I have ever seen. Her eyes are closed in an expression of pleasure, and her lips are drawn taut around the girth of my shaft. Just the sight is amazing, but the feeling of her tongue on me coupled with it?

It makes me mad with need.

I put my hand on her head, tangling in her mane. "Take your mouth off of me before I lose myself on your tongue."

She pulls back, surprised. "Did I do bad? Or something wrong? Or—"

"Nothing wrong," I assure her, and sink to my knees. I put my hands on her body, gliding up and down her back. The urge to touch her—to take her—is rising inside me. "It felt too good."

Her little giggle sounds pleased. "Gotcha."

"If I am going to spend, I wish to do so inside you." I lean in, capturing her mouth with mine.

"Oh," she says softly. "I want that, too." Her arms go around my neck, and she pushes her teats against my chest.

Kissing her, I bear her back down to the furs. Humans are smaller than sa-khui females, and I feel a bit of worry that I will be too big for her, in all ways. But Jo-see is smaller than Suh-mer, and she has borne two kits for her big mate, with another on the way. Surely there will be no problems.

Even so, I am cautious as I position my body over hers. I brace my weight on my elbows, careful not to crush her.

Suh-mer does not feel the same wariness I do—she eagerly wraps her legs around my hips and arches up against me. "I want you inside me, Warrek. No more waiting."

I nod. It is what I want. I rock my hips, dragging my cock along the wet folds of her cunt. She is slick with her need, and the feel of her is beyond pleasure. Her little moan as I do only makes me want to tease her more. I glide up and down, wetting my length with her juices. I do this until she is crying out my name, begging me to enter her. I want that. I want that more than anything. Even now, the sultry way she says my name makes my cock tighten, ready for release.

I pause to kiss her again, mating my tongue with hers. She responds eagerly, hungry for more, and she clings to me, her touch demanding. "Now," she whispers. "Now, now now now."

"Now," I agree, fitting the head of my cock against the entrance to her core. Tonight, we wait no longer.

I push at her entrance, but she is tight despite how wet she is. With another kiss, I pull back and decide to push into her with my fingers again, thrusting. She makes a small noise of protest, but her mouth is captured by mine, and she soon loses herself in the kiss. I continue to stroke my tongue against hers, thrusting in with my fingers. When she is even more slippery than before, I add a third finger, trying to stretch her.

"Warrek," she pants between kisses. "Please."

I nod and mount her again, determined to try once more. This time, when I push at her entrance, she gives way, and her little whimper at my invasion is followed by her digging her nails in.

"Don't stop," she tells me. "Don't stop until you're in all the way."

I groan, panting against her mouth. It is taking everything I have to go slowly. She is tight and narrow, and I fear I will hurt her. "We must go slow—"

"No," she tells me, trying to raise her hips.

"Stop," I caution. "Do not—"

"I don't hurt, Warrek. I want you in me, not just the tip. You can't break me, I promise!" Her hands are all over me, touching my cheek, my neck, smoothing down my shoulders. She meets my gaze. "I promise I'd tell you if something was wrong."

I nod. I trust her. I press my forehead to hers and push forward a bit more, ever so slowly. Her body seems to instinctively clasp mine, and when she makes no noises of pain or protest, I push deeper.

"Spur," she gasps. "Spur, spur, spur."

I freeze, worried I've hurt her. "It is a problem?"

"Oh, fuck no. It's the best thing ever." The look on her face is nothing short of bliss. "Oh god, do that *again*."

Thrust into her? I do so again—carefully—and she makes the most intriguing *squeal*. She likes it. I am pleasuring her. Relief courses through me, and I kiss her again with enthusiasm as I push into her once more.

When I realize I will not break her with my body, I relax and begin a rhythm, moving over her. Our hips move, and she pushes up when I thrust down, creating more friction between us. There is no sensation like that of her cunt clasping me tight, and it is the best thing I have ever felt. Normally I am quiet, but tonight, in her arms, I have no words to describe this. No words to say how I am feeling. I just rest my hand on her brow, gaze into her lovely eyes, and claim her body with my cock.

She trembles under me, and every time I thrust, she makes that soft half-squeal, half-moan, a shudder rocking through her. I can feel her desire rising, can feel her cunt tighten around my cock.

"Oh my god," she breathes between thrusts. "It's like you're hitting me in the money spot every time you move. I think a spur is my...new...favorite...thing." Her eyes widen, and she trembles around me. "Oh fuck!"

She comes and comes hard, her cunt clenching tight around me. I can feel every ripple of her pleasure through her body, and it squeezes my length and makes it impossible for me to stop. I growl low in my throat and bend over her like an animal, mind-lessly mating. The only thing in my world at this moment is her body against mine and the soft cries of her release. I cannot stop myself. I pump into her with all the need and urgency that has been building these many days, ever since we left the ship.

No—ever since she put her mouth on mine and kissed me. My cock has not gone down since.

Just thinking about that makes a tremble rip through my form, and I feel my sac tighten again, my body ready to release. This time I welcome it; there is no reason to hold back any longer. I let go, moving with fierce need as my release moves through me.

I realize dimly that I am roaring as I empty into her, filling her with my seed. It does not matter; the tribe knows she is mine.

Now they just know I can be as loud as her.

19

SUMMER

I sigh blissfully as I curl up against Warrek's sweaty chest in the furs. We're both still breathing hard, moments after we've both come. I'm a little sore between my legs, and I'm sure I'll feel it in the morning. I'm also sure I don't care in the slightest. That was beyond amazing. No wonder all these human women have the happiest smiles on their faces. They're getting spur every night.

Spur, and a big, ridge-covered dick.

This must be heaven.

"Hea-fen?" Warrek murmurs, rubbing his big hand down my back.

Oh, did I say that out loud? "Just commenting on how good that was," I tell him with a little yawn. I stretch, feeling catlike and sexy, and I love that he watches my boobs as I do. I've never felt particularly sexual in the past, but around him, I feel like a vixen.

And I'm also pretty sure I could go for that again, as soon as I catch my breath.

"I am glad it was pleasing to you." He slides his hand up my side, moving to my front to cup my breast, as if he can't help himself. "I wanted you to enjoy it."

"Oh yeah," I say dreamily. "You could say it was pleasing, all right."

He chuckles at my expression. "I am glad we took tonight for ourselves. It will help in the nights to come."

I smile at him and snuggle against his chest. It takes a moment to realize what he just said, and when I do, I sit upright. "Uh, what do you mean, it'll help in the nights to come? What's coming?"

Warrek looks at me thoughtfully. Oh, damn, a man should not look so sexy with strands of his own hair plastered to his skin, but he does. I want to lick all the sweat off his body. Maybe I will... once I find out what the heck he's talking about. "The upcoming journey back to the ship."

"There's an upcoming journey back to the ship?" I echo. Then I realize what I'm saying. "Oh, duh. Of course there is. We have to retrieve the others and figure out what to do with the pod people." I groan, resting my chin on his chest once more as I press up against him. Really, I can't stop rubbing up against the man. He's just so touchable with all those muscles and that blue suede skin. "Can't say I'm eager to go back out on the trail, though."

"Then it is good you are not going."

Say what? I sit bolt upright again, frowning at him. "What do you mean, I'm not going?"

He reaches out and lazily traces a circle around my nipple. "It will be hunters only. Vektal will not risk an unmated female going to the others or getting captured if another ship arrives. We will need to move fast, and we will need our strongest, bravest warriors."

"I'm strong," I protest. "I'm brave."

"You are both, my mate," he agrees, pulling me down against him. "But that does not change that you will not be coming." He rubs his nose against mine. "I will be happier knowing you are here and safe and dreaming of me and my spur every night."

A joke? Warrek made a joke? I'd find that downright adorable if I wasn't so miffed. "I don't want you to go," I tell him. "Isn't this kind of like our honeymoon? Can't you go on the next trip?"

He shakes his head. "My chief will need me. I am one of the few hunters that has no kits to feed. I am more free than the others. I would not be surprised if Harrec stayed behind, with Kate newly resonated to him. Bek will go, I think. He is eager for revenge against those that frightened his mate. And some of the long-mated hunters, I think. The swiftest ones."

So...everyone that's going has already resonated. And there are sixteen hot human ladies just waiting for their chance at big, blue-ridged dick and spur.

Oh, hell no. This one's mine. "I want you with me," I tell him stubbornly. "I need you here."

He touches my cheek. "I would love to stay and roll in the furs with you for days on end, my lovely Suh-mer, but the tribe needs me."

"And what happens if you leave my side and you resonate to someone else?" I protest. "What then?"

I'm surprised at the possessive look that comes over his face. He frowns and pulls me down against him. "Do not think such things."

"I can't help it. I—"

My words are cut off by his kiss. Hot, fierce, and utterly sensual, he slicks his tongue against mine and kisses me until I'm weak in the knees...and wet between the legs once more.

"You are mine, Suh-mer," he murmurs as he moves me underneath him and pushes my thighs apart. "My mate. No khui will determine this for us. You are mine and mine alone."

I can't argue with that.

20

SUMMER

I'm still thinking about it in the morning when I wake up and I'm alone in the furs, though. Just the thought makes me cranky. I had dreams all night about Warrek going to the ship, and a hot band of Playboy Bunnies bounded out, and they all resonated to my man.

Grr.

My Warrek hasn't been gone long, though. There's a large bowl of melted, warm-ish water by the coals of the fire, and I use it to splash myself clean, and then dress in fresh leathers. I can smell something cooking in the distance, and it makes my mouth water. I'm a little shy about going out in public now that everyone "knows" we're together, but I'm going to have to get it over with at some point.

I put on my boots, wrap a fur around my shoulders, and then peek out into the village. No Warrek. No hunters at all, actually. I see a few people camped out in front of their huts for their daily chores, but Kashrem's the tanner, and that doesn't count. Tiffany's seated near him with her own tanning frame, and her son Lukti even has his own pint-sized hide stretched on a small frame so he can work alongside his mommy. I swear, that's the cutest. Other than their small cluster, I see the elders stirring something in a pot, and another works on carving off on his own. No hunters. They're either out for the day...

Or all meeting with the chief.

The thought is a little distressing. I think about my dream with the Playboy Bunnies again and wrinkle my nose, frustrated. I don't want Warrek wandering around a bunch of single women. And man, if that doesn't sound like a cranky housewife thought, I don't know what does. But not with his cootie going rogue and refusing to pick a mate. He needs to stay away from them until the initial cootie frenzy gets taken care of.

When we first got here, Josie chattered on and on about how so many people resonated right away that it was practically a flurry of matings and that it must have had something to do with the new khuis searching for a mate immediately. At the time, it made me feel a little crappy, because when I got here, I didn't resonate to anyone. Out of all of us, only Elly did, and I felt like my cootie didn't think I was special enough to zoom in on someone.

Of course, now that I've met Warrek, I'm glad that my cootie has kept its mouth shut. But what if Warrek goes with the rescue party and resonates to someone else? I'll die inside.

Not because I've been left out or because I'm not special, but because I'll lose the best thing that's ever happened to me.

With those depressing thoughts in my head, I follow the delicious breakfast smells to the longhouse.

Sure enough, there's a crowd of women there, all hovering by the fire and talking in low voices. Stacy's got her weird-looking skillet in hand and is busy scraping something out of her pan when she glances up at me. "Oh, hi Summer," she calls out in a singsong voice.

All faces turn toward me.

Oh jeez. I can feel my face turning red, and an awkward smile tightens on my mouth. "Hey guys. Am I in time for breakfast? It smells great. Not that it doesn't always smell great. And if I'm too late, that's all right. I can always make my own." My speedy babble starts, and I want to smack myself in frustration, but I just keep yapping instead. "I totally don't mind. I was a latchkey kid and so I always had to make my own snacks growing up, but it was easier with a pantry, you know? Here you have to prep all your food yourself, and while I'm sure it's better for you because it's all organic, sometimes I wish for a Pop-Tart. You know, I visited a Pop-Tart factory once when I was a kid. Well, it wasn't really a factory as much as—"

Josie steps forward, parting from the cluster of women. She moves to my side and puts her arms around me, silently hugging me.

"Um, what's that for?" I ask, bewildered.

"For telling the men about the G-spot," she says with a happy sigh.

A chorus of giggles go up from the crowd of women. One of them is a sa-khui woman—Asha, I think—and she's got her little girl seated in her lap, gnawing on a not-potato cake. She just rolls her eyes, an amused smile on her face.

"Oh, I didn't say anything about that," I tell them, a little horrified that something so private got out. "I would never—"

"But you told Warrek about it, and he mentioned it to Harrec," Kate says, that dreamy look from the last few days still on her face. "And Harrec told everyone. And I do mean everyone."

"God bless you," Josie says, hugging me again. "I mean, that shit was good before, but now..."

"Now things got turned to eleven," Nora says, and puts her hands on her cheeks. "Am I still blushing? I feel like I'm blushing."

"I ran into Kira this morning, and she giggled like a schoolgirl," Maddie adds. "Funniest thing ever."

I try to picture serious Kira giggling. "Um, really, I'm not sure you should be thanking me—"

"It never occurred to me to give Raahosh an anatomy lesson," Liz continues, snatching the next cake from Stacy's skillet before Stacy can slap her fingers away. She takes a bite out of it, then says, "I mean, I normally just indicate I wanna have sex and let him go to town. One-way trip to orgasm-ville. Between the spur and the ridges, I thought it couldn't get better."

"Eleven," Nora says primly. "Definitely an eleven."

Claire and Ariana just giggle wildly.

"Sounds like everyone had a good night," I begin.

"Not as good as you," Josie says in a sly voice. "You guys should have picked a hut farther out in the village."

"How far can they go?" Lila asks, rubbing her big, pregnant belly absently.

"The coast, I'm thinking," Maddie says dryly. "Maybe then we won't hear what they're up to."

I keep smiling, even though this is just as bad as I thought it would be. "Okay, well, this is a great conversation and I think I'm going to go die of embarrassment now."

"Oh, stop," Josie says, putting an arm around my waist. "You think you're the only one that's been a bit noisy during sex? Feel sorry for Farli and Asha for having a hut next to Maddie and Hassen."

Maddie just snorts. "Like I care. Newsflash, I'm attracted to my mate."

"Come sit," Josie says, steering me toward the fire. "We're not trying to freak you out. It's just been...an eye-opening experience for some of us."

Ariana giggles again.

"Here, have a pancake," Stacy tells me, pouring a new batch of goop onto her skillet. "Well, it's kind of a pancake. It's a not-potato —or notato as I'm calling them lately—ground into a powder and mixed with some of the ground-up hraku seeds. It's not perfect, but it's sweet and hits that pancake urge if you ever have one, like me." She grins over at Asha and her little daughter. "Shema likes them."

"Shema likes everything," Asha says, smoothing her kit's hair back from her tiny horns. "Yesterday I caught her gnawing on one of Hemalo's boots. She had eaten the laces before I stopped her."

"Sounds like my girls," Nora says wistfully. "They chewed the hell out of everything when they hit their terrible twos. I'm looking forward to that again." She pats her flat belly and beams. "Only a year and some change to go."

"And are you ready to be a mom?" Lila asks Kate.

Kate goes pale, her face matching her hair for a moment. "I'm not sure," she admits. "It's not like I get a choice, of course, but I haven't pictured myself as a mom before."

"I didn't either. You get used to it." Ariana offers her a smile.

"I wish I had a few more years to get used to the idea," Kate says. "Sometimes I'm excited, and sometimes I wish I was like Summer. She's lucky her khui's staying quiet for now."

Yeah, lucky. Lucky that my man is going to go to a ship full of nubile Earth women just raring to put their hands on a sexy sa-khui man. I'm so lucky that I'm going to lose my guy to a stranger.

At the thought, I burst into tears.

The cheerful banter immediately stops. The longhouse goes quiet, the only sound the sizzle of the pancake in Stacy's skillet.

"Here," Asha says, handing me a leather cloth. "Wipe your face and tell us what is the matter."

"I didn't mean to make you cry," Kate speaks up, aghast. "I'm so sorry."

"It's okay," I sniffle, wiping my face with the cloth. "Well, no, it's really not okay or I wouldn't be crying. I'm just emotional, I guess."

"Because of Warrek?" Asha guesses. Stacy holds out a plate with the pancake on it, and when I hesitate, Asha clucks, gesturing. "Eat. Eat and tell us what the problem is. We are all your friends here."

I guess they are, even if Asha's mothering me like her little daughter. Still, it's nice to not feel so alone. And the chagrined expression on poor Kate's face tells me she didn't realize what she said. I take a bite of the steaming hot pancake. There's no syrup, but it's sweet throughout and does taste more like a pancake than a cookie. "It's good. Thanks, Stacy."

"I'll make you another," she says soothingly, turning back to the fire. "You just take your time and eat."

I do eat, though it's not easy with a bunch of women giving me worried glances. I feel like a dork for crying, but every time I think of the situation and picture my sweet, quiet Warrek resonating to some new chick, I just get a huge knot in my throat.

"I think I'll see how the twins are doing with Mr. Fluffypuff," Nora says, getting to her feet. She gives my shoulder a squeeze as she walks past.

"I'll come," Kate adds, and mouths an "I'm sorry" to me as she follows behind.

I nod, shoving pancake in my mouth. I'm not mad at her. I just hate the situation. The others are sitting around, watching me, and when my pancake is gone, Asha gives me an expectant look. Right. I'm supposed to tell them what's bothering me. "I just...we just found each other, you know? And now he's going to leave with Vektal and all the other hunters, and there's a bunch of fresh women in the pods, and what if he resonates to one of them? I love him so much, but what if we're not meant to be together? What if his cootie takes one look at some hot new thing and it decides that she's the one for him?"

"Then the khui decides," Asha declares. "That is how it works."

"I don't think that's going to make her feel better," Lila murmurs.

"Does she want to feel better, or does she want the truth? You cannot deny resonance." Asha shrugs.

Asha's right, but it doesn't fix the knot in my throat. I wish I knew what to do. Something. Anything. I feel helpless in the face of this looming disaster.

"You cannot stop resonance," Asha continues, noticing my silence. "But that does not mean you do not have choices."

I glance over at her. "Oh?"

She nods. "For many seasons, I was paralyzed by my own dark thoughts. I did nothing to go after my happiness. It took much to change my thinking. Then I realized the only person standing in the way of what I wanted was me." She smooths Shema's hair again, a smile curving her mouth. "You can choose to sit back and let things happen, or you can do something about it."

Do something about it? But she just said that you can't stop resonance. I frown in her direction. If he goes, I can't exactly put a shield around his cootie and say, "Not now, big guy." And even if I go with him, that doesn't change that he might resonate to someone else.

But if he doesn't go...

I sit upright. I can't stop things if his cootie is going to resonate to someone else at some point. But if he doesn't go, maybe I can stop him from being there when those initially boy-crazy cooties go off like rockets. If he's safely tucked in my bed, maybe by the time they get to the tribe, they'll be all done and there will be nothing to worry about.

"You don't know that they're even going to wake them up," someone says.

I'm not listening any longer, though. I get to my feet, inspired. "I think you're right, Asha. I think I'm going to do something about it."

But first, I need to talk to the chief.

21

SUMMER

*O*f course, because I'm unlucky, the chief isn't home.

Georgie is, though. She's lying in bed, a puke bucket near her face. Her oldest daughter, Talie, strokes sweaty hair back from her mom's forehead, and the younger is playing in one corner of the hut.

"Is this a bad time?" I ask from the doorway. "Because if it's a bad time, I can come back."

"Nah, it's fine." She sits up, putting the bowl between her folded legs. "Talie, honey, why don't you go see Kate's kitten again? Take Vekka with you."

Talie gives her mother a dubious look. "Are you all right?"

"I'm fine, baby girl. Go play." She manages a bright smile.

I add a quick, "I think the twins were playing with him a few minutes ago."

Georgie shoots me a grateful look, and the girls give their mom kisses and then race out the door, past where I'm standing. "Thank you. It worries them to see Mama sick. They don't realize that this is expected. Talie was too young to remember much about me being sick with Vekka, though I admit this is a different kind of fun."

"Oh?"

She nods and gestures at a seat near the fire. "Come sit. I'll stay in bed if you don't mind."

"I don't mind." I move to the stool, watching her. "This pregnancy different than the others?"

"In little ways. The puking started earlier. And when I was pregnant with the girls, I wanted to eat everything in sight. Now any sort of raw meat turns my stomach. Not exactly a great thing, given where we live."

I have to laugh at that. It took me a while to get used to the fact that the sa-khui eat raw meat constantly. "That is a bit difficult."

"Gonna be a lot of eggs for the next fourteen months or so." She makes a face and then leans over her bucket again. "Or not," she adds faintly.

Oh dear. "Can I get you anything?"

She shakes her head, still leaning forward. "Just tell me what's up. Distract me."

"Oh. Okay. Well." I wring my hands as she makes gagging noises and try not to sympathy-puke. "I wanted to see if there was a decision about waking up the humans or not. I guess I'm just being a bit nosy. You don't have to tell me if you don't want to. And I can totally see myself out if I need to. You don't have to get up. I totally understand if it's not something you want to talk about—"

She puts a hand up to stop my nervous yakking. "Summer, it's okay. We can talk about that. I mean, everyone owes you. Warrek talked about how brave you were. He told Vektal all about how you pretty much had a plan for everything and you put yourself at risk to save the others. He was so impressed with your bravery."

I feel a little flustered at the flattery. "I just did what anyone else would have done."

"Maybe. Either way, the tribe can't thank you enough."

"So...have you guys decided?"

Georgie sighs. "Yes and no." She lies back down on the blankets, fluffing her pillow. Her face is sweaty, and she's pale, but she sets the bucket down next to the furs and isn't heaving anymore. Progress. "It's ultimately Vektal's decision. He's the chief. But he's also...well, he's innocent." She frowns to herself. "All of these people are. If you tried to explain war to them, or murder, they don't get it. To them, all people are a great big happy family that get along. Sure, we argue, but the worst thing you can do to someone is ignore them for a few days. And we all saw how well that went with Bek, right?" She grimaces. "But you and I know not everyone is nice. Not everyone is in this for the common good. I have to be the negative one sometimes. And that means I have to shoot down some of his ideas."

My stomach feels like it's tied in a fierce knot. "Oh?"

She stretches on the blankets, then pulls them over her. "It's funny, you know. I've never wanted to be a leader. Never wanted to be in charge of anything. And I was pretty sure that when I was a mom, I'd be the cool mom, you know? The laid-back one who doesn't take anything too seriously. Turns out that now I get to be a leader—or a co-leader, at least—and I'm not the cool mom at all. I'm the helicopter mom who overprotects everyone and freaks out over everything. But...I have to. I feel like I'm responsible for my girls, for the others in the tribe, and especially the humans here. It's like I'm mom to everyone." She rubs her brow. "Sometimes it's a little stressful and I make snap decisions that aren't always the right ones. But I try to think of everyone and how the entire tribe is affected. So yeah. I'm not the cool mom. I'm the one who makes you eat all your carrots before you get up from the table, and then if you make too much noise, I'm going to make you sit in the corner for three hours and think about what you've done."

"This is a hard job," I say quietly, giving her support. "I don't know that anyone would want it."

"Mmm. Vektal loves being chief, though. I guess it's different when you've been groomed for it all your life. And when you have a really innocent view of the world." Her smile is faint.

All of Georgie's talk makes me worry a little. "So...we're not getting the newcomers out of their pods?" I don't know how I feel about that. On one hand, I feel a tiny kernel of relief. On the other, I feel horribly sorry for those trapped people.

"Oh, we're getting them out. Sorry. My mind is wandering. I was up all night talking it over with my mate." She rubs her eyes with the back of a hand. "But I admit, a lot of me didn't want to. Part of me still wants us to run screaming in the other direction. It's the helicopter mom in me acting up again. I want desperately to protect my family, and the tribe is my family. It's just..." Her eyes look suspiciously glassy. "I lost everything once, you know? My planet, my life, my family. If I lost it again, it'd break me. Maybe that's why my knee-jerk reaction is to say no." She sighs. "But at the end of the day, they're people, and they need our help, so we're going to help them and hope they're not convicts or murderers."

I swallow hard. Jeez. Here I was just worrying that they were too sexy. Georgie's taken worry to a whole new level. "If that's the case, then I want to ask that Vektal tell Warrek that he can't go."

"Warrek cannot what?" Vektal ducks into the hut, a steaming bowl in his hands. His gaze flicks to me, and he gives me a quick nod of greeting before moving to his mate's side. He kneels by the furs and strokes Georgie's tangled, sweaty curls. "I brought you broth. You must drink this. You need your strength."

She nods and sits up, giving him a grateful smile full of love. "Thank you, love." She cups the bowl and takes a sip, then tells him, "Summer and I were talking about the newcomers. How we're worried, but it's still the right thing to do to save them."

He nods firmly. "There is no other choice. We will welcome them and feed them. There is room enough for all."

Georgie shoots me a look, and I remember what she said about the sa-khui being innocent. She's not wrong. What if these are bad guys? I don't blame her for wanting to protect her "family."

"I want Warrek to stay here." I plunge ahead bravely. "I know you guys need every strong hunter to go and help with the rescue party, but here's my thing. He hasn't resonated, and I think if he goes, he's gonna resonate to a newcomer. It'll cause all kinds of problems, and I'm sure everyone would prefer that doesn't happen, you know? Especially me."

Vektal gives me a patient look. "Is that so?"

"Yes." I'm pretty sure his lips are twitching with amusement, but I continue. "I know it's a thing with hunters dragging the woman they've chosen off to a cave because they want to hold her until they resonate. I've heard all kinds of stories about that, and apparently Raahosh did it with Liz, right? Or Maddie and Hassen? I don't remember the details. Kate and Harrec ran off for a while, too. At any rate, I want to do the same to Warrek. I want to kidnap him."

"You do?" Vektal looks astonished.

"I do."

Georgie giggles into her broth. "I'm picturing oh-so-serious Warrek being kidnapped by a small human woman."

"Well, it's more like I'll tie him up and keep him in our hut for a few days." I blush, because it sounds kinkier out loud than it was in my head. "Just long enough that he can't catch up with the rescue party. Not that I don't think it's a noble thing to do. I..." I swallow hard. "I think my heart would shatter if he came home with a new mate."

"You cannot force resonance," Vektal says, but his gaze is on Georgie as he says it, and he's devouring her with his eyes. It's clear he wants her as much now, all sick and sweaty, as he did the moment he met her.

"I know that. I just want him to avoid that initial mating surge. And maybe give us a few more days together. Like a honeymoon."

"Ho-nee-moon?" Vektal echoes. "Again?"

"Yup. Again." She pats his arm. "But different this time."

"And you wish for Warrek to stay behind?" Vektal grins.

"I do." I try to sound brave and determined like everyone thinks I am, but I'm about to shake with nervousness. "I want to kidnap him."

"It is not necessary," Vektal says. "My Georgie and I decided last night that we would only send mated hunters on the retrieval party in order to avoid such a situation as you have described. We do not need newly mated strangers adding that to our list of problems. Both Sessah and Warrek will stay behind."

"Oh." Well, that took all the steam out of my argument. "I see."

"But," Georgie says with a little smile on her face. "I think you should kidnap him anyhow. Rattle him a little. Show him what's what. And I'd bet money that he wouldn't mind being tied up by his woman for a honeymoon."

I grin at her, and I'm already planning out my strategy. If Warrek wants to think of our relationship as chess, I'm about to put his cute, tight ass into checkmate.

22

WARREK

*T*he hunters of the village are hard at work, bringing in last-minute kills and preparing their weapons for the chief's rescue hunt. The village was deserted this morning, but we have flooded back in with the setting of the twin suns and will spend late into the night getting ready.

I think of Suh-mer. I want nothing more than to crawl into the furs and hold her close until the suns rise once more and I must leave her. But there is much to do this night, and I must help the tribe. So many lives depend on it. I cannot be selfish.

"Have you seen our chief?" Sessah asks, ducking into the long-house. Normally this is a friendly gathering spot, but tonight, it is filled with hunters preparing their packs and readying weapons for the trek into the wild tomorrow. "He is not in his hut."

"He is somewhere in the village," I tell him, stretching a long length of thin leather to bind several spears together. "He will be here soon."

"Warrek?" A voice calls my name and I glance up from the bundle of spears I am lashing together. It is Hemalo, wiping his hands clean of filth from an afternoon of scraping leathers. "There you are," he says when his gaze meets mine. "Asha said that Suh-mer is looking for you. It is urgent."

A hint of fear courses through me. Urgent? "Is she unwell?" I drop the spears I am bundling, and they clatter to the stone floor, scattering everywhere. Sessah looks up at me in surprise. Normally calm, I find I am flustered, grabbing one spear only to have another drop away. The thought of Suh-mer calling for me because something is wrong tears at my mind.

"I will finish that," Sessah offers, giving me a curious look. He scoops up the spears scattered at my feet. "Go and see to your female."

I nod, rubbing a hand down my face. "I thank you." I turn to Hemalo. "Is she in our hut? Did Asha say anything more?"

"I believe she is waiting for you at the edge of the village," he comments in a mild voice, unruffled at the sight of my clumsiness.

I nod again, then realize I am just bobbing my head over and over at this point. With that, I head out of the hut, my thoughts scattered and wild. Is Suh-mer sick? Has she hurt herself somehow? Is that why Hemalo was sent to find me? My stomach churns at the thought of leaving her to journey with the others, but it is something I must do. I cannot abandon my people, and she is safe here.

But the thought of leaving her behind? It fills me with a helpless frustration and a deep-seated, gnawing hunger that feels foreign to me, almost as foreign as the overwhelming lust I feel at the thought of her, smiling over her shoulder at me.

Or smiling at another hunter. What if, while I am gone, she decides she wants a different hunter in her furs? One as talkative as her? Sessah is closer to her age, for all his youth, and the new hunters we will pull from the pods will be looking for mates.

I nearly double over at the jealousy that rakes through me.

I never thought of myself as one to snarl at another male glancing at my mate. But never has another female consumed my thoughts like Suh-mer has. What would my father say, I wonder, as I race through the village, looking for the sleek dark mane of my human. Would he even recognize his son?

Perhaps he would. Perhaps he would encourage me to capture every moment with Suh-mer. I remember how keenly he missed my mother when she was gone. He would understand why I feel so strongly.

And he would be happy for me.

A hard knot lodges in my throat at the thought of my father, gone these last few seasons. He would have liked my Suh-mer and her endless talk. He would have admired how brave she is. How clever. And he would tell me not to let her get away. That I should spend every day making her feel cherished, like my father did my mother.

It is something I vow to do...just as soon as I find her.

I stalk past a cluster of the human females, barely noticing that they giggle as I leave. They are not Suh-mer, so they are not important. Not right now.

"Warrek?" her sweet, familiar voice calls nearby.

I whirl about. There she is, standing in the doorway of one of the storage huts at the very edge of the village. She waves me forward, one arm hidden behind the doorway.

Relief courses through me at the sight of her. She does not look injured. "What is it?" I ask, and my voice is louder than it perhaps should be. "What is wrong?"

She just waves me over again. "Come inside. We need to talk."

Talk? She is not injured? There is an odd look on her face that concerns me, but as long as she is well, I can deal with everything else. I move to her side, ducking into the hut, and cup her cheek. "You are not hurt? Not injured? Not feeling ill? Shall I call the healer?"

Her expression goes soft. "Oh, it's nothing like that. I'm sorry to have scared you." She keeps her hand carefully behind her back as she tilts her head up and gazes at me. "Can I ask you to do something for me?"

"Of course." I stroke her cheek, unable to stop touching her. She is just so beautiful it makes my heart pound in my chest as if I have been racing along the trails all afternoon. I love her flat human face with its small nose and funny brow. I love her golden skin and her slight body. I even love her tail-less bottom. I especially love the way she smiles up at me, like I am the best thing she has ever seen. It is how she smiles at me right now, and my heart pounds even harder.

"Then can you close your eyes and put your hands by your side?"

It is a strange request, but for her, I will gladly do whatever she likes. I nod and do as she has asked, my hands lowering to rest and my eyes closed.

"Boy, Georgie was right," she murmurs to herself. "You guys are seriously innocent. Hold still, baby." I feel her body graze against me. It feels as if she is circling around me, and when she runs a hand under my leather vest to brush her fingers over my stomach, my cock rises at the simple touch.

I am so distracted by her that I barely notice she has pulled something taut around my torso until she gives it a yank. "When can I open my eyes?" I ask, curious.

"When I'm finished tying you up."

That...is not what I expect to hear. I open my eyes, curious, and see that she's tied a thick leather band around my upper arms. She grabs another band and ties this one around my waist, pinning my arms at my side. There is a look of great determination on her face as she works.

"Why do you tie me up?" I am amused at her efforts, and a little confused. It would not take much to wrestle my way out of the bonds, but I am curious as to why she feels the need to put them on me.

"I'm kidnapping you," my Suh-mer announces. "I already got the chief's permission and everything. I'm going to kidnap you and hold you hostage in the cabin here for the next few days and have my wicked, wicked way with you." She smiles up at me and wriggles her eyebrows.

Now I am truly confused. "You have the chief's permission to tie down my arms?"

"Well, no, that part was my idea." She grabs another bit of braided rope and flings herself around me, winding the cord along my waist. "See, I thought the other sa-khui guys kidnapped their women and toted them off to a cave post-resonance, right? I wanted to do that with you even though we haven't resonated.

We're still mates, and it doesn't matter to me if we ever resonate. But resonance wasn't the whole reason I wanted to tote you off, you know? Not that I can tote you off, of course. You weigh, like, twice as much as I do, and it'd be a bit like a housecat trying to carry off a lion. Or a bobcat, I guess, instead of a housecat. Because if our sizes were really that big of a difference, sex would be a hell of a lot more uncomfortable. So yeah, I guess bobcat and lion. I saw both of them at a zoo once, and you don't realize how big a lion is until you see it up close and personal. That's how I feel about your dick sometimes." She giggles. "Lion-dick. The others will think I'm crazy if I tell them that. Not that I would, given all the ribbing they threw at me with the whole G-spot thing. No regrets there, though." She sighs happily and ties the cord into a big floppy bow. "None at all."

"You have my heart, my mate," I tell her gently. "But I have no idea what you are talking about."

She chuckles again and tugs on the ties at my waist, pulling me forward a bit. "Long story short—though I guess it's too late for that—I'm kidnapping you here, and you're not going to leave for days."

I slowly shake my head. "I would love to roll in the furs with you for nights on end, but the tribe—"

"Has already decided that both you and Sessah are staying behind because you're unmated, and they don't want anyone's cootie going off like a firecracker on the Fourth of July. There's enough to deal with, you know?" She slides a hand down the front of my leathers and cups the bulge of my erection. "Which means you and I get time to play."

I am surprised to hear this. Her hand is distracting, but I force myself to stay focused, even when she traces the outline of my cock with her fingers. "Vektal...has decided we shall not go?

When did you hear of this?"

She bites her lip and tilts her head. "When I went and asked them not to send you?" She winces. "I hope you're not mad."

I am astonished—and strangely pleased—at her boldness. "Why would I be mad?"

"Because if you really wanted to go, it's not my decision—"

"I do not wish to go," I tell her quickly. "I would rather be with you. But if the tribe needs me..."

"Not half as much as I need you." She strokes my cock again, causing the breath to hiss from my throat. "And maybe I'm a horrible beast, but the thought of you resonating to someone else while I'm sitting back here makes me crazy. I'm far too possessive of you to let you get away."

I can feel a grin spreading across my face. My heart is pounding wildly at her words, at her touch on my cock. She feels this strongly about me, as well? "Then I am not alone in being jealous at the thought of others getting your attention?"

"You're jealous over me, too?" she gasps, delighted. "Oh my god, that's so cute. I love it." Her hands glide up and down my shaft, and I bite back a groan. Suh-mer seems so very pleased. "Something like that deserves a reward."

"You are my reward," I pant. "I want nothing else."

"Seriously, I am going to eat you with a spoon." Her hands tug at my loincloth. "You're making my heart race with all this talk."

Her heart is racing as well? Mine seems to be going faster and faster with every moment that passes. It thunders in my ears, and my world seems to be shrinking to her hands on my cock and the pounding in my chest.

But then...I hear it.

A low, throbbing hum coming from my breast.

Resonance.

23

SUMMER

*T*ouching Warrek is making me absolutely crazy this day. Maybe it's something about him being tied up and helpless in my arms. Maybe it's the fact that I'm "kidnapping" him. Maybe it's his sweet, sweet words that are making me melt quicker than ice cream in the desert, but I swear I'm about to come out of my skin if he says one more sexy thing to me. I'm already pressing my thighs tightly together, and my nipples are hard under my tunic.

I feel flustered and wild and...throbbing. It's the strangest thing ever.

"Resonance," Warrek says in a hushed voice. "Such a gift."

I don't understand what he's saying. Is he...is he sad he won't get the gift of resonance if he doesn't go? "What do you mean? You want to go so you can resonate?" And me with my hands on his *cock*?

He laughs, twisting in his bonds. "No. Suh-mer. Listen to your chest. Listen to your khui. Listen to mine if you do not hear it."

What...oh.

Oh.

I'm not feeling antsy or nervous. I'm not throbbing...my cootie is. We're resonating. "Oh, Warrek! It happened for us!"

"Yes. My heart sings along with my khui." He twists in the bonds again and then growls, baring his teeth. "Take these off me. I wish to touch you."

I put my hands on the leather bindings, intending to do just as he says, but I'm all flustered and hot with the realization of what this means. Resonance. Us.

Babies.

Us. Together. Forever.

Babies.

My babies with Warrek. We're going to be a family.

I give a little happy squeal and bounce, holding on to his front. "Warrek! We resonated!"

He chuckles at my happiness. "I know, my heart. Now take these bonds off of me so I can claim you as mine." His laughter dies, and his look grows strangely intense. "I want to fill you with my seed."

Oh, wow. I press my thighs tight together, but I'm totally slippery between them. A breathless moan escapes me, and I forget all about anything except touching him. "You're supposed to be my captive," I tell him. "Why would I free you? I'm having such fun." My cootie purrs up a storm, making me feel all flustered and breathless inside...and aroused. Is this how everyone feels when their cootie kicks in? This intense need paired with jitters, like you're going to fall apart unless you touch the other person right now now now?

If so, no wonder there's such a huge fuss over resonance. No wonder it's so devastating when it's with the wrong person. No wonder it's so terrifying. I feel like I've lost all control of who I am, because in the space of a minute, I've gone from Summer to Warrek's forever mate and a mother to be. I've also gone from playfully turned on by touching him to wildly aroused and full of need. My pulse has started pounding squarely between my thighs, and I feel like if we don't have sex in the next few minutes, I might lose it.

He growls, clearly of the same mindset, and shifts in the bonds again. "Let me go."

"Let you go?" Dear lord, is that husky, sensual voice mine? "I'm tempted to just throw you down and have my wicked way with you."

He freezes in place, and I swear I can see his eyes darken with lust. Oh wow, he likes that idea.

Oh man, I do, too.

"Lean down and kiss me," I whisper.

He does, his lips brushing over mine. As they do, I grab the front of his leggings and undo the laces on his loincloth, pulling it free. His cock surges free, and I gasp to touch his scorching hot flesh. I drag my fingers down the ridges, endlessly fascinated by them. I never thought something like that would make a big difference, but when he pumps into me, I can feel every bit of him, and it's mind-blowing.

His breath hisses out between his teeth, and he leans in and nips on my lip this time. "Free me," he murmurs.

"I've got a better idea," I tell him. I hook my fingers in his leggings and drag them down his big, muscled thighs. "How about you sit down and I crawl into your lap?"

His muffled groan tells me he likes that idea almost as much as I do. Gracefully, he drops to his knees and then falls back onto the furs I have spread on the floor for such an occasion. He tilts his head and leans forward, pulling his hair free from where it was trapped under him, and then he's sitting on his butt in the furs, legs crossed in front of him. His cock thrusts up from his lap, ready and gleaming with precum.

All the while, my cootie's thrumming and singing as if it wants the entire tribe to hear what's happening between us. And Warrek's is just as loud, his song a little lower-pitched than mine but no less urgent.

Breathless, I peel my leathers off, enjoying the way he watches me. He looks ravenous, as if he'd eat me alive if I got any closer. Then again, I know what his mouth can do, so maybe that's not an inaccurate statement. For a moment, I consider pushing him onto his back and sitting on his face like a wanton hussy, but the cootie's demanding dick, and who am I to disappoint? I toss the last of my leathers aside and step forward, naked. He's still seated upright in the furs, upper body all bound in my ties and his lower body naked except for his boots. It'd be kind of funny if I wasn't so aroused right now. Nothing matters but getting him inside me. Nothing.

"I love you," I tell him breathlessly as I drop to my knees and move closer, putting my arms around his neck.

"My heart," he murmurs, gaze intense. "My mate."

"All yours," I tell him, and I mean it. It feels like everything that's happened was meant to bring us together. Like we're the two people most right for each other in the whole world—in several worlds. Maybe I did have to leave Earth and come to the far ends of the galaxy just to meet him. It's a fair trade-off.

He nips at my mouth. "Climb onto my cock, my heart."

Oh, were ever such dirty words so sexy? I moan, holding on to him and doing just as he asks. It's a little awkward to put my legs over his hips, but he knows my body intimately, and he's had his face—and tongue—all over every inch of it. There's no need to be embarrassed, not when it's just us. And the way he looks at me? I'm the sexiest thing in the world and he's letting me know it. So I take him in hand and guide him to my opening, pushing the head of his cock against my core. Then slowly, slowly, I sink down on him.

We're both breathless as I move over him. All the tension in my body is building so quickly I feel as if I'm going to come before I even get him fully inside me.

But then I'm seated fully on his length, and his spur is pushing against my clit. We're face to face, my breasts pressing to his chest, and this easily feels like the most intimate embrace we've ever had.

This moment is special. Amazing. Intense.

Perfect.

He kisses me again. "You will have to move for both of us," Warrek murmurs.

I nod. It makes sense. He's using his core to hold himself steady, but he won't be able to lift his hips up without knocking both of us to the ground. So I hold on to him and experimentally lift up and then sink back down onto him.

Both of us groan as I do. It's the most incredible thing, and my cootie is purring so hard it feels like my entire body is vibrating.

It's doing fascinating things to my insides, and when I slide down onto him, it almost feels like he's vibrating, too.

I whimper and do it again, then again, my movements jerky and frantic. I'm full of need, and I don't care if this is the shortest round of sex we ever have, as long as I come and come soon. His breathing is raspy and quick, and I know he's thinking the same thing.

Then his hips shift, and he's thrusting with me somehow, even though I'm the one on top. I bury my hands in his hair and frantically move up and down on him, rocking my hips wildly in my need to come.

I explode a scant moment later, my body shattering, and my cry of release almost feels as if it's been drowned out by the constant song emanating from our khuis. Warrek breathes my name and leans in, burying his face against my shoulder, and then I can feel his body tremble with his own release. We practically came together.

Well, almost. The timing wasn't perfect, but I'm sure it's something we can work on. We have forever to perfect this kind of thing. And as I kiss his sweaty face and rock my hips over him, I can't help but smile.

Forever with Warrek sounds like heaven.

"My brave, perfect mate," he murmurs. In his eyes, maybe I am all those things.

I don't care as long as I'm his.

EPILOGUE

BROOKE

"*B*uh-brukh, are you all right?" Farli gives me a curious look over her shoulder. "You seem angry this day."

I grit my teeth. I don't bother correcting her that my name isn't "Buh-brukh" but "Brooke." They never say my name right anyhow, and thanks to my stutter when someone first asked my name, Buh-brukh has stuck. Everyone calls me that, and at this point, I usually don't mind.

Of course, Taushen calls me Brooke, but Taushen can also jump off a cliff for all I care.

I shrug, braiding her hair a little tighter. I may not be a great huntress, and I'm not terrific with electronics, but being a hairdresser means I can make a fierce braid, and Farli likes my efforts, so I make it a point to do her hair every day. Today I'm doing a starburst coronet of braids—not so easy with someone that has a pair of horns. But her hair's so thick it's going to look downright magnificent when I'm done. "Just thinking."

"Are you...what is the word." She pauses for a moment. "Like Ell-ee? Your head hurts after what we endured?"

Is she asking if I'm traumatized? It's sweet of her to worry. Truth be told, the alien hijack and almost-kidnapping was scary, but it had a good ending. We're still here on the ice planet. It was actually less traumatic than my last experience. No one stripped me naked and prodded me or checked my teeth. No one pinched my flanks or sniffed my hair or groped me. No one stole me away from everything I've ever known.

Except for one particular incident, it actually went much better than expected when one's captured by slavers. "I'm okay," I tell her, glancing up when someone comes into the space ship. It's only Rukh, though, and I concentrate on braiding again. "I'm not going to go all Elly and not bathe for months if that's what you're asking."

She chuckles. "I was merely curious. You have been less...friendly with Taushen. I wondered if he said something cruel."

Oh, did she notice the chill between us? I grab another section of her thick hair and weave it into her thick braid. "It wasn't anything he said," I edge.

It was definitely something he did, though. The dick.

As if our thoughts have summoned him, Taushen enters the spaceship hold next. We're seated just inside the Tranquil Lady, at the top of the ramp, because Farli's pet llama-thing is pawing at the snow below and nipping at frozen roots underneath. She wants him to stay close, but since he was pooping all over the deck, we decided to set up here so I could do her hair.

Of course, that means we're in a high traffic area. And that means the hunters are coming through, and that means Taushen has wandered near. He's got a spear in hand, a hopper corpse in the other. He nods at Farli and gives me a cold look. "Buh-brukh," he murmurs, then saunters past.

Oh, burn. That ass. I know very well that he knows how to say my name correctly. He said it just fucking fine when he was balls deep inside me.

But I suppose that's my fault, too, since I'm the one that seduced him.

Farli hisses, pulling away. "You are making my mane a very tight cord today."

Oops. "Sorry. I'll pay more attention." I pat her shoulder and try to forget all about Taushen, or that night in the ship. It didn't mean anything, just like I told him then.

No idea why he's continuing to be a huge dick about it. I'm pretty sure these people are familiar with the concept of 'one and done'. And I'm pretty sure that the situation we were in was an obvious one that meant no strings attached. And the sex was good. Really good.

But for some reason, Taushen's had a burr up his butt ever since.

And if he's expecting me to go to him and apologize for seducing him to save both of our lives? He's going to be waiting a long, long damn time.

AUTHOR'S NOTE

Hello again!

Oh, my sweet barbarians, how I've missed you! Maybe it's just the way that my schedule has fallen, but it feels like this book has been waiting forever to come out. Between dragons, Prison Planet Barbarian, and my secret NY stuff, I've been away from our tribe for far too long. I'll try not to let that happen again. As a result, though, I think you'll notice this book packs a bit of a punch. There's a romance (of course, this is me we're talking about here) and a lot of shenanigans going on over on our favorite ice planet.

I'll never mess up a happy ever after for a couple, but that doesn't mean that strange and exciting things won't happen to our tribe!

Still, I hope this book makes you as happy as it made me. I've got plans for the future coming out the wazoo (sounds painful) and you can look forward to many, many more books with our tribe. I've thought about going forward in time, going backward...but I think we're going to stay right here for now and see what happens. I hope that's all right with all of you.

I've gotten feedback about how people were unhappy with Georgie and how she's acted in the more recent books, so I've tried to show a bit of her perspective on things. While we might not always agree with what she decides, her heart is in the right place, and I hope even if you don't like her decisions, you understand them a little better. And if you still don't like her...that's allowed, too! I've always felt that a tribe is going to have people that annoy us at times but we still love them - just like family.

I've also heard that some readers were unhappy that there was less 'guy' point of view in the more recent books. I try to go with whoever feels natural for the scene, but you'll see in this one that Warrek stars just as heavily as Summer...though he might say a little (okay a lot) less than she does. I'll try to keep this in mind for future books, too.

I get a lot of questions about audio - there's still no audio (yet) for barbarians, but dragons will be coming out this summer. If there's another question I'm missing and you're dying to have answered, feel free to hit me up on my Facebook author page.

I'm sure you're wondering what's next - I've already started Brooke's book. It doesn't have a title yet. My working title is Barbarian's Pink, just because I'm drawing a blank. Maybe I'll take suggestions over on Facebook!

(But please, not in email, because I never check the darn thing...)

After Brooke's book, we'll swap back to dragons and Emma's story. Still to come in the future: Gail's story, more dragons, Kivian's story (Jutari's brother!), and I've even got a story brewing for poor, almost-forgotten (not really!) Ariana. No word on Marlene yet. She's a cagey one to pin down.

All in all, it's going to be a busy next few months. I'm looking forward to it.

<3

Ruby

THE PEOPLE OF ICE PLANET BARBARIANS

As of the end of Barbarian's Rescue (8 years post-human arrival)

Mated Couples and their kits

_____

Vektal (Vehk-tall) – The chief of the sa-khui. Mated to Georgie.

Georgie – Human woman (and unofficial leader of the human females). Has taken on a dual-leadership role with her mate. Currently pregnant with her third kit.

Talie (Tah-lee) – Their first daughter.

Vekka (Veh-kah) – Their second daughter.

_____

Maylak (May-lack) – Tribe healer. Mated to Kashrem.

Kashrem (Cash-rehm) - Her mate, also a leather-worker.

Esha (Esh-uh) – Their teenage daughter.

Makash (Muh-cash) — Their younger son.

———

Sevvah (Sev-uh) – Tribe elder, mother to Aehako, Rokan, and Sessah

Oshen (Aw-shen) – Tribe elder, her mate

Sessah (Ses-uh) - Their youngest son

———

Ereven (Air-uh-ven) Hunter, mated to Claire

Claire – Mated to Ereven

Erevair (Air-uh-vair) - Their first child, a son

Relvi (Rell-vee) – Their second child, a daughter

———

Liz – Raahosh's mate and huntress.

Raahosh (Rah-hosh) – Her mate. A hunter and brother to Rukh.

Raashel (Rah-shel) – Their daughter.

Aayla (Ay-lah) – Their second daughter

———

Stacy – Mated to Pashov. Unofficial tribe cook.

Pashov (Pah-showv) – son of Kemli and Borran, brother to Farli, Zennek, and Salukh. Mate of Stacy.

Pacy (Pay-see) – Their first son.

Tash (Tash) – Their second son.

———

Nora – Mate to Dagesh. Currently pregnant after a second resonance.

Dagesh (Dah-zhesh) (the g sound is swallowed) – Her mate. A hunter.

Anna & Elsa – Their twin daughters.

———

Harlow – Mate to Rukh. Once 'mechanic' to the Elders' Cave. Currently pregnant after a second resonance.

Rukh (Rookh) – Former exile and loner. Original name Maarukh. (Mah-rookh). Brother to Raahosh. Mate to Harlow. Father to Rukhar.

Rukhar (Roo-car) – Their son.

———

Megan – Mate to Cashol. Mother to Holvek.

Cashol (Cash-awl) – Mate to Megan. Hunter. Father to Holvek.

Holvek (Haul-vehk) – their son.

———

Marlene (Mar-lenn) – Human mate to Zennek. French.

Zennek (Zehn-eck) – Mate to Marlene. Father to Zalene. Brother to Pashov, Salukh, and Farli.

Zalene (Zah-lenn) – daughter to Marlene and Zennek.

———

Ariana – Human female. Mate to Zolaya. Currently pregnant. Basic school 'teacher' to tribal kits.

Zolaya (Zoh-lay-uh) – Hunter and mate to Ariana. Father to Analay.

Analay (Ah-nuh-lay) – Their son.

———

Tiffany – Human female. Mated to Salukh. Tribal botanist.

Salukh (Sah-luke) – Hunter. Son of Kemli and Borran, brother to Farli, Zennek, and Pashov.

Lukti (Lookh-tee) – Their son.

———

Aehako (Eye-ha-koh) –Mate to Kira, father to Kae. Son of Sevvah and Oshen, brother to Rokan and Sessah.

Kira – Human woman, mate to Aehako, mother of Kae. Was the first to be abducted by aliens and wore an ear-translator for a long time.

Kae (Ki –rhymes with 'fly') – Their daughter.

———

Kemli (Kemm-lee) – Female elder, mother to Salukh, Pashov, Zennek, and Farli. Tribe herbalist.

Borran (Bore-awn) – Her mate, elder. Tribe brewer.

———

Josie – Human woman. Mated to Haeden. Currently pregnant for a third time.

Haeden (Hi-den) – Hunter. Previously resonated to Zalah, but she died (along with his khui) in the khui-sickness before resonance could be completed. Now mated to Josie.

Joden (Joe-den) – Their first child, a son.

Joha (Joe-hah) – Their second child, a daughter.

———

Rokan (Row-can) – Oldest son to Sevvah and Oshen. Brother to Aehako and Sessah. Adult male hunter. Now mated to Lila. Has 'sixth' sense.

Lila – Maddie's sister. Once hearing impaired, recently reacquired on *The Tranquil Lady* via med bay. Resonated to Rokan. Currently pregnant for a second time.

Rollan (Row-lun) – Their first child, a son.

———

Hassen (Hass-en) – Hunter. Previously exiled. Mated to Maddie.

Maddie – Lila's sister. Found in second crash. Mated to Hassen.

Masan (Mah-senn) – Their son.

———

Asha (Ah-shuh) – Mate to Hemalo. Mother to Hashala (deceased) and Shema.

Hemalo (Hee-muh-low) – Mate to Asha. Father to Hashala (deceased) and Shema.

Shema (Shee-muh) – Their daughter.

———

Farli – (Far-lee) Adult daughter to Kemli and Borran. Her brothers are Salukh, Zennek, and Pashov. She has a pet dvisti named Chompy (Chahm-pee). Mated to Mardok. Pregnant.

Mardok (Marr-dock) – Bron Mardok Vendasi, from the planet Ubeduc VII. Arrived on *The Tranquil Lady*. Mechanic and ex-soldier. Resonated to Farli and elected to stay behind with the tribe.

———

Bek – (Behk) – Hunter. Brother to Maylak. Mated to Elly.

Elly – Former human slave. Kidnapped at a very young age and has spent much of life in a cage or enslaved. First to resonate amongst the former slaves brought to Not-Hoth. Mated to Bek. Pregnant.

———

Harrec (Hair-ek) – Hunter. Squeamish. Also a tease. Recently resonated to Kate.

Kate – Human female. Extremely tall & strong, with white-blonde curly hair. Recently resonated to Harrec. Pregnant.

———

Warrek (War-ehk) – Tribal hunter and teacher. Son to Eklan (now deceased). Resonated to Summer.

Summer – Human female. Tends to ramble in speech when nervous. Chess aficionado. Recently resonated to Warrek.

Unmated Elders

———

Drayan (Dry-ann) – Elder.

Drenol (Dree-nowl) – Elder.

Vadren (Vaw-dren) – Elder.

Vaza (Vaw-zhuh) – Widower and elder. Loves to creep on the ladies. Currently flirting with Gail.

Unmated Hunters

––––––

Taushen (Tow – rhymes with cow – shen) – Hunter. The cheese stands alone. Womp womp.

Former Human Slaves

––––––

Gail – Divorced older human woman. Had a son back on Earth (deceased). Approx fiftyish in age. Allows Vaza to creep on her (she likes the attention).

Brooke – Pink-haired human female. Former hairdresser. Not a fan of Taushen.

IPB READING LIST

IPB Reading List

Are you all caught up on Ice Planet Barbarians? Need a refresher? Click through to borrow or buy!

Ice Planet Barbarians – Georgie's Story

Barbarian Alien – Liz's Story

Barbarian Lover – Kira's Story

Barbarian Mine – Harlow's Story

Ice Planet Holiday – Claire's Story (novella)

Barbarian's Prize – Tiffany's Story

Barbarian's Mate – Josie's Story

Having the Barbarian's Baby – Megan's Story (short story)

Ice Ice Babies – Nora's Story (short story)

Barbarian's Touch – Lila's Story

Calm - Maylak's Story (short story)

Barbarian's Taming – Maddie's Story

Aftershocks (short story)

Barbarian's Heart – Stacy's Story

Barbarian's Hope – Asha's Story

Barbarian's Choice – Farli's Story

Barbarian's Redemption – Elly's Story

Barbarian's Lady - Kate's Story

Barbarian's Rescue - This story!

Next up...
Brooke's Story (title TBA)

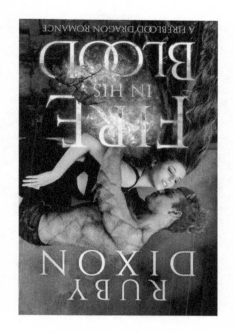

Ruby does dragons! Have you tried it yet? Click on the cover to borrow!

FIRE IN HIS BLOOD

Years ago, the skies ripped open and the world was destroyed in fire and ash. Dragons - once creatures of legend - are the enemy. Vicious and unpredictable, they rule the skies of the ruined cities, forcing humanity to huddle behind barricades for safety.

Claudia's a survivor. She scrapes by as best as she can in a hard, dangerous world. When she runs afoul of the law, she's left as bait in dragon territory. She only has one chance to survive - to somehow 'tame' a dragon and get it to obey her.

Except the dragon that finds her is as wild and brutal as any other...and he's not interested in obeying.

What he is interested in is a mate.

WANT MORE?

For more information about upcoming books in the Ice Planet Barbarians, Fireblood Dragons, or any other books by Ruby Dixon, like me on Facebook or subscribe to my new release newsletter. I love sharing snippets of books in progress and fan art! Come join the fun.

As always - thanks for reading!

<3 Ruby

PS - Want to discuss my books without me staring over your shoulder? There's a group for that, too! Ruby Dixon - Blue Barbarian Babes (over on Facebook) has all of your barbarian and dragon needs. :) Enjoy!